BRUSHSTROKES

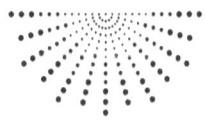

TONI BLAKE

To Michelle, for the inspiration,
to Lori, for the encouragement,
and to LuAnn, for a nudge in the right direction

CHAPTER ONE

*I*t was a bad day to be lounging in the bathtub.

It was an even worse day to be lusting over a man she didn't know.

It was Mia Drake's thirtieth birthday.

Lifting a bubble-covered foot from the water, she used her toes to twist the antique faucet off. She should be back in New York celebrating with her friends. She should be hitting her usual Lower East Side haunts, badgering the manager of her favorite Orchard Street gallery to look at her work. But instead she found herself in tiny Sassafras, South Carolina, soaking in her Great Aunt Clara's old clawfoot tub, pretending a few bubbles and the scent of an aromatherapy candle would make everything better. And if that wasn't bad enough, she was thinking dirty thoughts about Rick Rose, the brawny dark-haired bar owner she'd seen in town.

She lay her head back on the edge of the tub, indulging fully in the simple but effective fantasy. *The bathroom door opens and she looks up. It's him—all strong, sexy six feet three inches of him. Neither seems surprised to see the other; his eyes*

1

burn with a knowing, confident desire that makes her shiver despite the warm water. His gaze lands on her bare breasts, her nipples jutting through a thin film of suds, and she feels his look everywhere. Her breasts turn heavy, needy, beneath his scrutiny.

"Am I intruding?"

"No," she replies, her voice as smooth as melting butter. "In fact, I was just thinking about you, wanting *you. Come into the tub."*

He strips off his clothes with swift, sure movements, revealing a muscular chest, a great butt, and an incredible erection that makes her feel empty and achy between her thighs. She wants to wrap her hand around his length, caress him. No, more than that. She needs him to fill her.

Sadly, she'd never even met the man. She'd just seen him around—standing outside his bar chatting with locals, driving his heavy duty pickup truck up Main Street, eating in the local diner, and once in the grocery store when she'd stopped to get some cherry tomatoes for a salad Aunt Clara was making. The mere sight of his face—all serious gray eyes and commanding jawline—had delivered the same sensations she experienced now.

She'd had a hell of a time selecting her tomatoes while imagining those strong arms closing around her, those big hands touching her. He struck her as a bit gruff—it was something in his eyes, something in his voice on the few occasions she'd heard him speak—but that didn't seem to lessen the effect he had on her. She'd lingered over the tomatoes until he'd collected a few ears of corn and an onion, then gone on his way.

After he eases into the water behind her, she leans back against his broad, muscular chest. His hands come around to cup her wet breasts as his hot arousal presses into the center of her ass, making her rub against him. Turning her head, she draws him down into a delicious tongue kiss that adds to their indelible heat. As he caresses her sensitive breasts, squeezing her taut nipples ever-so-slightly between his fingers, his raspy voice comes as a whisper near her ear. "Ride me."

Of course, there were worse things than coddling herself with a little birthday fantasy. And certainly worse things than living with Aunt Clara for a while, until she got back on her feet. The truth was, if she'd stayed in New York, she didn't know where she'd be right now, but it probably wouldn't *really* have equated to that fun, buzzing-about-the-city birthday she'd just envisioned. Five out-of-work artists sharing a loft hadn't added up to a rent payment, let alone a birthday party. She was only thankful her aunt had always been so welcoming. It had been a huge comfort to have someplace to go where she didn't feel like a burden. When Aunt Clara's last letter had come, bearing the line, "I can't stand to think of you living in poverty, and I would love having some company around this old place," Mia had done the only practical thing. She'd packed her easels and canvases and brushes into the old family SUV she'd never gotten rid of, and she'd headed south for the winter.

Now it was almost spring, though, and what had she done for herself? Painted a lot, yes. Found a way to make some money? No. And despite her sweet old aunt's endless love and generosity, the guilt of freeloading weighed on her. She had to earn her keep and earn it soon.

But…not right this minute. It was her birthday, after all. And there was an imaginary man in her bathtub who needed to be ridden.

Turning, she straddles him in the water. His hands find her breasts again and she glances down to see his fingers capturing the mounds of flesh, a few remnants of white bubbles peeking through. His slow, firm massage turns her breath thready as she looks into his eyes. They meet hers; they own her. Gripping the white porce-

lain with both fists, she leisurely slides the swollen, open juncture of her thighs up and down the column of stone between his legs. They both release light moans of pleasure—but he's impatient, planting his hands on her hips, positioning her for entry, murmuring one demanding word. "Now." Then he pushes her down.

A knock came on the door and Mia flinched. For a fraction of a second, she actually expected Rick Rose to be on the other side. But then Aunt Clara's soprano tone echoed through the old wood. "Mia? Are you in there?"

Inside, she groaned. *Fantasy killer.*

"Yes," she said. "I'm taking a bath."

"Well, have a good, relaxing soak, dear. I simply wanted to let you know I'm home. When you're done, we'll have a nice birthday lunch on the back veranda and I'll tell you what I found out in town today."

Mia looked toward the door. Her imaginary lover wasn't the only one in this tub who was impatient. Not that she suspected her aunt really had anything *big* to tell her, because what could Aunt Clara have discovered in town that would particularly interest Mia, someone who didn't even belong here? "You can't tell me now?"

"You just take your time and enjoy your bath, dear."

Sure, easy for Aunt Clara to say. She hadn't had a totally splendid tub fantasy doused with a huge splash of cold water just when things had gotten really hot. Besides, she could hear her aunt puttering around the old house now, humming while she worked on lunch. There was no hope of sinking back into her sexy vision at this point.

With a sigh, she used her toes to, this time, flip the old-fashioned handle that opened the drain, then stood and reached for a towel. *So long, imaginary birthday sex.*

Drying off, she let out a long sigh. Sad when it came to this. Thriving on fantasies. Clearly, it had been too long since she'd had a *real* man.

Maybe this was the universe's way of kicking her in the butt. Making her realize that if fantasizing about a stranger is the best thing you have to do on your birthday, something's wrong. And since when was she the sort of person who got all caught up in fantasies anyway? There'd been a time—a few mere months ago—when life had been too busy, too active, too everything—for her to sit around getting bored enough to drool over a man she didn't even know.

Yep, this was a wake-up call, all right. Back in New York, she'd seen thousands of people every day without focusing unnaturally on one particular stranger. Here, not so much. She clearly had too much time on her hands, too much time for idle wanderings of the mind. So sure, maybe this could be explained by not having had a boyfriend in a while—but it could also be explained by...not having had much of a life since coming to South Carolina.

Ten minutes later, she'd changed into jeans and a T-shirt, and she pushed through the back screen door of the quaint white clapboard cottage to find Aunt Clara waiting at a wrought-iron patio table. The older woman had made dainty finger sandwiches of ham salad, as well as deviled eggs and baked beans, all served on old-fashioned plates and bowls with roses circling the rims. Cups of tea had been poured and a small birthday cake set perched on an antique pedestal at the table's center. The bright sun of the early March day only added to the warmth that filled Mia. It had been a while since anyone had done anything this special for her birthday.

She smiled lovingly. "Aunt Clara, you're too good to me. This looks wonderful." So wonderful that, despite it being just the two of them, she felt a smidge underdressed. But it was nice to discover she actually did have something better to do on her birthday than fantasize in the bathtub.

Her aunt's face wrinkled around her grin, and eyes still as blue as the ocean shone beneath silvery hair, pulled back into a bun. "Now, you know I like having someone to do nice things for. It's been too long since I've had a proper tea party, and this seemed the perfect occasion."

As the two women sat and enjoyed the lovely lunch, Mia drank in the salty Carolina sea air, thoughts still lingering over how much she appreciated Aunt Clara's presence in her life. Mia had lost her parents in a car accident seven years ago, and since then, her mother's aunt—which, of course, actually made her Mia's *great* aunt, but that was too much of a mouthful—had become her touchstone.

They'd not known each other well while Mia was growing up—Aunt Clara and her now departed husband Frank had lived down here in the Carolinas, "in a little town by the ocean," her mother used to say, and Mia's family had resided in upstate New York. Yet when the devastation of her parents' death had driven her to drop out of grad school and head to the city in reckless pursuit of her dream to be an artist, Aunt Clara had been there for her, with phone calls and letters and care packages—as well as plane tickets to South Carolina for a week every summer.

The cottage, decorated with aging gingerbread trim, was surrounded by weeping willows and large old oaks draped with Spanish moss. A thin, sandy beach lay only a short walk away past marshes and an inlet that often teemed with cranes, egrets, and occasionally even a small alligator. Sassafras had become a home away from home for Mia—so different, quiet, even isolated compared to the Big Apple.

Sometimes she wondered if she'd been trying to hide by going to New York, by becoming one of the thousands of struggling artists who practically blended into the city land-scape. Now she couldn't help but wonder if she was hiding *here*, in the proverbial middle of nowhere. She'd been in Sassafras for over two months without earning a dollar,

letting her aunt support her. Somehow Aunt Clara's uncon-
ditional love made Mia's lack of direction painfully apparent.
As did turning thirty. For her, the age signaled full-fledged
adulthood.

Your twenties is when you find yourself, make your way
in the world, get established. By her thirties, she'd expected
to have done those things and...be somewhere. Well, somewhere besides living off the kindness of a relative.

Even as she listened to Aunt Clara talk about the things
she'd done and people she'd seen this morning in town, Mia
found herself feeling as if she were at a fork in the road.
Maybe it was time to grow up, time to be practical and take
responsibility for her life. Maybe it was time to give up
the dream.

"Where are you, dear?"

Mia lowered the deviled egg between her fingers to her
plate. "Hmm?"

Her aunt's eyes turned pensive. "Your body might be
sitting here with me, but your mind is someplace else."

True enough, but Mia didn't want to admit her troubling
thoughts. Aunt Clara would only pour on the sympathy, and
that's not what she needed right now. What she needed
was...fortitude, and the will to make herself do something it
would be easier not to: quit feeling sorry for herself and
make some practical life decisions. "Just thinking about my
birthday," she replied. "Just thinking that this is something
my mom would have done for me. Thank you, Aunt Clara.
For everything." She hoped her aunt understood the full
measure of her gratitude. "Now—what were you going to tell
me?" But she loved Aunt Clara, but she didn't love being
mushy, so she was ready to move on from that.

"Oh me," her aunt laughed. "I'd nearly forgotten already.
But I ran into someone who's looking for a painter."

"Looking for a painter?" Hmm. Mia had the feeling Aunt Clara might be barking up the wrong tree here.

The old woman nodded. "A sweet young man I've watched grow up over the years, along with his brothers. He needs someone to paint the interior of his tavern. You know, the one on Main? The place belongs to Rick Rose."

Mia couldn't have been more stunned to hear her bathtub lover's name on Aunt Clara's lips. What were the chances? Never mind that he wasn't a man who struck her as even slightly sweet, and that Sassafras was apparently an even smaller town than she already thought—was her aunt actually suggesting she work for him?

"Generally, the Snapply family takes care of most folks' painting needs around here," Aunt Clara went on, "but Pete Snapply's down with a broken ankle and his boys are backlogged something fierce. I heard Rick say he's in awful need of a paintjob, has been for months, but he doesn't have the time to do it himself. During the days, he helps at his parents' nursery out on Highway 45. So when he said he was looking for a painter, I told him my great niece was a painter, and that I'd put you in touch with him."

Mia quietly digested this new information about Rick Rose. Up to now, he'd been only a name, a face, a body. Okay, one hell of a face and a body. But someone to think about in an almost abstract, this-isn't-real kind of way.

Now he suddenly had a family, a second job, a life with practical needs and concerns—like having walls painted.

Not that any of that mattered, though—because…"Aunt Clara, I don't do that kind of painting."

Yet the old woman shrugged. "Painting is painting, isn't it? Colors, brushes." She narrowed her brow and leaned forward slightly. "I worry about you, dear, being stuck inside this house all the time. I think it would be good for you to get out, start a new project."

And make some money. Mia knew that wasn't Aunt Clara's motive, but this *would* be a paying job, a way she could contribute to household expenses while she figured out what to do next. And painting some walls wouldn't require much concentration; the task would give her plenty of time to figure out her next steps in life.

Of course, other than having painted the occasional room, she didn't have the faintest idea how a painter—*that* kind of painter—worked. But how hard could it be? And it would also provide her with a first: she'd make money from painting.

The harder part would be actually approaching Rick Rose, fantasy bathtub stud, and someone she'd never expected to have any dealings with outside her own mind.

MIA CHECKED her watch as she traversed the sidewalk toward the Rose Tavern, its windows the only ones lit up on Main Street. The dulled sounds of laughter and talk mixed with Bruce Springsteen's "Glory Days" growing louder as she approached.

It was ten thirty. At night—because the bar wasn't open during the day. Yet why had she waited so late to come, rather than showing up at, say, sevenish, which struck her as a more seemly time to discuss a business transaction? Probably because she'd spent the evening trying to talk herself out of it, trying to tell herself she'd go see him tomorrow, or maybe next week. But then she'd reminded herself that ambitious, determined people didn't put things off, and that she really wanted to repay Aunt Clara for her generosity, at least as much as she could.

Clearly, a lively Friday night crowd had gathered and it probably wasn't the most conducive time to pitch her painting services to Rick Rose, but that was too bad. As she opened the heavy wooden door, the previously-muffled noises blared in her ears, and more than one eye turned her way. A few people appeared vaguely familiar from around town, but most were strangers. This was obviously a place where everybody knew your name—unless you were a temporary resident in Sassafras, and one who stuck close to home while here, like Mia.

The men studied her approvingly while women, on the other hand, seemed to glare. She was invading their territory —albeit unwittingly. She still wore blue jeans, but had traded in her tee for a casual yet fitted low-cut tank top that showed off a few curves. If she was going to have a one-on-one with her bathtub fantasy man, she wanted to look good.

She made her way to an empty barstool, still aware of the curious glances, even as people went on with their conversations and laughter. And for the first time a question hit her. What if he was married? Or had a girlfriend? For some reason, she hadn't even wondered before—but the women in the bar had just reminded her of things like competition and jealousy. And maybe she hadn't bothered to wonder until now because up until this moment, he'd been only a passing fantasy. Having to ask that question was one more thing that took him out of fantasy realm and made him real.

She spotted him easily just then; he stood behind the bar, at the opposite end, flirting with two brunettes, one of them wildly overdressed—or was that underdressed?—in a stretchy skin-tight leopard-print dress, the fabric sprinkled with bits of metallic gold.

"Kelly Ann, what are you doing in here dressed like that?" Rick Rose asked, adding a rich, baritone chuckle. Despite the remonstrance, his tone said he didn't mind the view.

"Lookin' for love, sugar." Kelly Ann flashed suggestive eyes and leaned slightly over the bar to give him a closer glance at her cleavage, as if he couldn't see enough flesh already.

"In all the wrong places?" he asked.

She shrugged. "You know I'm not a stickler for right and wrong."

He laughed and gave her a wink. "And that's exactly what I like about you."

They were sleeping together, Mia just knew it. Ugh.

"Hey Rose, you got a customer down here."

Mia flinched as the middle-aged man two stools away hiked a thumb in her direction. "Uh…thanks," she murmured.

As Rick turned to look her way, her body blossomed with the same mind-numbing awareness he'd brought out in her at the grocery store. Only this time she instantly envisioned him naked, beneath her in an antique bathtub. A shiver snaked through her, especially when his dark eyes pinned her in place as if she were a butterfly in a collection case. And when she least expected it, his gaze left her with the same powerful sensations she'd experienced in the fantasy: possession, sexual ownership.

Okay, this was officially crazy. She was taking the images in her mind too far, and had definitely gone too long without a lover.

Even so, one thing was clear—the man was a walking, talking chunk of raw sexuality. He hadn't noticed her in the vegetable section, but he was definitely noticing her now. And crazy or not, the mere knowledge made her nerve endings hum with a desire that felt almost dangerous.

Approaching, he leaned confidently against the bar, his predatory gaze never leaving her. "What's your pleasure, sweetheart?"

She considered being offended and telling him she wasn't his sweetheart—she'd never appreciated the presumption of being called honey or baby by a man she didn't know. Or on the other hand, maybe if she were smart she'd just take the cue and say, *You. Right here. On the bar. Closing time.* Instead, though, she just swallowed nervously and replied, "I'll have a Bud Light."

Her fantasy man popped the top on a longneck and set it before her. "Glass?"

She shook her head. "Bottle's fine."

Still studying her in an unnerving way, he crossed strong arms over his snug navy blue t-shirt and tilted his head slightly. "Have we met?"

Kind of. I ogled you over fresh produce last week. She took a sip of her beer and set it back down. "No."

He leaned his head in the other direction, his gaze still intense. Never before had a man's mere look had such an effect on her. Her skin tingled and her breasts ached; she could almost feel her nipples puckering in her bra. And the longer his eyes examined her, the more real the sensations from her fantasy became. "I could swear I've seen you around. Are you sure I don't know you?"

She took a deep breath, then followed an impulse. "Yes, I'm sure, but *I* know *you*. And I have a proposition for you."

A few chuckles and one low whistle from nearby reminded her that she was on a stage here, suddenly the main event of the evening in Sassafras, South Carolina. Having their very first conversation with an audience wasn't fun, but she'd have to roll with it.

One corner of Rick Rose's mouth curved upward—not quite a smile, but enough to say she'd surprised him and that he was enjoying the game. "I should warn you, this won't be the first time I've been propositioned by an attractive woman."

"I don't doubt it."

"So let's hear what you've got to offer."

"In private," she told him. "Do you have an office or something?"

A few more snickers filtered through the smoky air, but she kept her eyes on the man before her. His expression grew a little closer to a smile now, the skin around his eyes crinkling slightly. "Sure, sweetheart. Follow me."

CHAPTER TWO

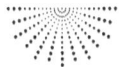

$\mathcal{T}$he woman following Rick toward the storage room was the freshest thing to hit Sassafras in years. Despite her promise of a proposition, though, she didn't strike him as the kind of girl ready to lean him back against a wall and have her way with him, at least not this fast. She and Kelly Ann were in different leagues. But he was still damn intrigued.

Actually, he'd been intrigued from the moment he'd taken in those bright eyes and the smooth, sun-kissed complexion that told him she wasn't accustomed to spring on the South Carolina coast. Her hair hung in thin, messy, honey-colored spirals that made him instantly want to run his fingers through it, and her lips had that swollen just-been-kissed look. What the hell kind of proposition could this woman have for him?

Stepping into the back room, he flipped a switch, illuminating the dim bulb overhead, then closed the door behind them, shutting out the crowd. Although he hadn't planned it, the move pinned her into a corner near towering shelves filled with cases of beer. He found himself instinctively taking advantage of that, placing one palm on the wall above her and peering down into pale blue eyes. She smelled of lavender. And despite himself, that quickly, he was a little turned on by her, that fast.

Despite her denials, he knew he'd seen her somewhere around town. "So, who are you, sweetheart, and what brings you into the Rose Tavern?"

Meeting his gaze boldly, she didn't seem to mind his nearness. "I'm Mia Drake and I want to paint your bar. My Aunt Clara Winstead sent me."

He blinked. This was Clara's great niece? Hell, he'd never in a million years expected someone so...sexy. Clara was a sweet little old lady, and for some reason he'd vaguely envisioned her niece as some younger version of her—short, stout, chatty. He couldn't have been further off the mark.

And he couldn't think of a worse idea than hiring this woman to work for him.

For one thing, lust and labor made poor companions. And for another, the girl came with baggage. Clara hadn't told him much, but he knew her parents had died and Clara was the only family she kept in contact with. In fact, she was staying with Clara and, as far as he could tell from his conversation with the older woman, had no place else to go. "I can't help being concerned for the dear girl," Clara had told him today as they'd talked at Millie's Diner up the street.

Of course, if he'd thought the lovely, fresh-faced Mia was interested in a casual roll in the hay, he'd be ready, willing, and able to oblige her. But already, just knowing what he knew, he had a feeling she wasn't that kind of woman—even if she *had* come into his bar sounding brassy and sassy. And if there was one thing important to Rick when it came to women and sex, it was keeping things light and casual. That's precisely why he got together with Kelly Ann from time to time, even if not as often as she came prowling for it.

At thirty-five, he'd had enough surprises in life, and he liked knowing what to expect. Despite the banter, Kelly Ann wasn't really looking for love, and that suited him fine. Comparatively, Mia Drake was an unknown quantity, so even if he was drawn to her, exploring that attraction seemed like a lousy idea. Plus, she was Clara's niece, a sweet woman he wouldn't want to risk offending by seducing and/or hurting her niece. It was time to tamp down that arousal and keep things simple here.

"Hate to tell you this, but you don't look a damn thing like a painter." He should take his hand down from the wall. And he should sure as hell quit staring at her like a thirsty man eyeing a tall, cool glass of water. But he didn't.

For the first time, she looked a bit ruffled. "Well, I *am* one." She tugged nervously on the hem of her top, the gesture smoothing the fabric snug across ample breasts. A hint of nipples shone through the outline of her bra and made him thirstier still—or hungry was more like it, for a taste of what lay underneath. So much for tamping down his lust.

"What have you painted?"

It caught him off guard when she let out a small disgusted-sounding sort of sigh. Simple question, after all. "Rooms. Plenty of rooms."

"Do you have any references?"

He didn't think it an out-of-the-ordinary request, but maybe it was his tone that had her looking disconcerted. "Look," she said, "I'm broke and I need a job. And it's my birthday. What do you say you cut me a break?"

He sighed. Already she was coming at him with a sob story. "All right," he heard himself say anyway. "You're hired."

She flinched, her eyebrows rising. "I am?"

In response, he stood before her equally as surprised. Since when did he say the exact opposite of what he was thinking? But he couldn't take it back now. He shook his head helplessly. "Yeah, sure."

Aw hell. Maybe it was because Clara was too sweet to disappoint. And it *was* the girl's birthday, after all—and he wasn't a *complete* ogre.

This just meant he had to institute an unspoken policy, right now, this minute—a *hands-off* policy.

That would have been a lot easier, though, if Mia's wide smile hadn't beamed clear through him just then, bright as rays from the South Carolina sun. "Thank you," she said, sounding completely different now. "Thank you so much!" A surprising innocence punctuated her gratitude, which felt sincere. Both the gratitude *and* the innocence. Enough that the her previous sassiness suddenly felt to him like an act. Bravado. And *that*—shit—somehow made her even more sexy.

"I won't let you down," she said—and in her new enthusiasm, she lifted dainty hands lightly to his chest. Then just as quickly removed them, her face flushing. "You won't be sorry, I promise."

Damn, he hoped not. That one little touch was currently ricocheting its way through his body like a bottle rocket. And it would be so easy to drop his hand to the curve of her waist, so easy to press her back into the wall with a warm, slow kiss. He looked down into her eyes as need bubbled up inside him, nearing the boiling point now.

What the hell was going on here? What on earth was drawing him to this woman so strongly? He thought again of her being an unknown quantity. Sassy or innocent—what was real and what wasn't? It all spelled danger, but also excitement. And she was sure as hell mooning up at him as if she wouldn't mind a physical connection herself.

But it was time to start putting that policy of his into effect once and for all, damn it. Maybe when the job was done, maybe when she was ready to leave town and go back to wherever she came from…maybe.

For now, though, no way.

"So when do you want me? To start?" she added softly.

His stomach clenched with desire. If she hadn't added those last two words, he'd have been a goner. "Early Monday morning," he said, forcing his mind back to business. "And you'll need to work quick, because I'll have to close the bar until you're done. I want to reopen by next Friday night, at the latest. I can't afford to lose weekend business."

She nodded. And he realized how close to her he still stood.

Then he finally found the strength to back away— although the hardness behind his zipper didn't thank him for it.

As if taking the cue, she moved toward the door, reaching for the worn brass knob. Yet as she opened it and the noise from the barroom came rushing in, she turned back to him. "Do you…have the proper equipment?"

He arched one eyebrow. *For what I want to do with you? Oh yeah, I've got the equipment.*

"I mean," she went on, sounding nervous, "scaffolding and drop cloths and that sort of thing."

Her words left him a little dumbfounded and shook him from his lust. "No, sweetheart. Already bought the paint—it's right there." A collection of gallon paint cans set on the floor next to an old desk. "Everything else usually comes with the painter. Don't *you* have it?"

She swallowed visibly. "I'm on the road right now— couldn't bring it all with me."

On the road from *where* when you have no place else to go? Of course, maybe she didn't realize he knew that part— or other things Clara had told him. Regardless, a painter having no equipment sounded a little sketchy. "Well, you can rent whatever you need at Hamler's Hardware on the corner."

Her look was doubtful. "But I'm broke, remember? As in…seriously broke."

The words reminded him: sob story, baggage. *Distance. Keep your distance.* "Put it on my tab with Bob Hamler," he said, "and I'll deduct it from your pay."

"Speaking of which," she said, pausing to reach down into the front pocket of her faded blue jeans to pull out a crumpled five-dollar bill, "I owe you for the beer."

"It's on the house." He suddenly didn't want any more physical contact with her—not even to take the money from her hand. It was time to remind them both that this was all business, nothing more. "I'll see you Monday morning at nine. Now I have to get back to the bar."

"Wait," she said as the moved to go.

He stopped, looked back.

"What color?"

He blinked. "What color is what?"

"The paint."

He blinked again. What the hell did it matter? "Off-white."

Was he imagining it or did her nose just scrunch up into a slight sneer?

"Anything else?"

She hesitated before finally saying, "Um, no."

"Good." And with that he walked out the supply room, left her standing there, and got back to where it was safe— where there was a room filled with Kelly Anns, a room filled with temptations that didn't tempt him half so much as the mysterious, sassy, innocent painter he'd just unwittingly hired.

~

LATE THAT NIGHT after the bar had closed, Rick lay in bed in his small frame house a few blocks off Main, windows open, drinking in the vague scents of salt and jasmine on the breeze as he tried to fall asleep. It would be easier if visions of Mia Drake weren't still dancing in his head.

He could have taken Kelly Ann up on her offer to get under that tight, shiny dress of hers—hell, he could have taken any of a number of women home tonight if he'd had a mind to—but he wasn't in the habit of satisfying a lust for one girl by being with another. So here he lay, unable to drift off, despite that it was after three a.m. and he was exhausted.

Clara's niece had stayed on his mind after she'd left, but only now, in the private silence of his home, did he have the opportunity to really envision what might have happened if he'd kissed her when he'd wanted to.

He could almost feel their bodies coming together, every-thing sturdy and hard about him pressing into everything soft and curvy about her. He could feel her warm skin beneath his hands, his fingertips skimming up her sides beneath her top, closing over her breasts—no bra. (It was a fantasy—she didn't have to have a bra.) He took possession of those two full globes of soft flesh, her firm nipples grazing the sensitive skin of his palms. And then her jeans were gone, fantasy-quick, and he was lifting her onto his old metal desk in one corner of the storage room, parting her legs, entering her with one smooth, sure, solid stroke. *Yes*.

That was when the sound of Silas Carter's barking dog cut into his near-sleep thoughts, shattering the imaginary ecstasy.

His eyes jolted open in the dark, taking in shadows on the walls. Damn it, why was he torturing himself like this?

To get her out of my system, that's why. One or two good fantasies and it would be almost the same as if it had really happened—right? And then he could forget the attraction and move on.

Okay, that was an exaggeration—a *wild* and maybe even almost silly exaggeration—but he'd have to try to make it work that way. Having her around his bar for the next week would be much easier if he could look at her without seeing someone he wanted to get naked with.

However, as the dog quieted and he rolled over in bed, another sleepy thought entered his brain. He could just follow his impulses and make a move on her. He could let himself enjoy her, forget his worries, forget tomorrow or the next day, and just indulge. She wouldn't say no.

Or would she?

She'd looked just as ready as he'd felt, but was the sensuality he sensed in her real or only in his imagination? After all, she'd seemed to go from tigress to kitten with him in a heartbeat when he'd awarded her the job. Maybe it was *all* just an act—get him hot, get the job.

And the main impediment here remained: If they did have some fun between the sheets—or on his battered old desk—she might expect it to matter, to mean something.

He knew better than most that needy women were trouble. The last needy woman in his life had taught him that the hard way. It had been years ago, but it had stuck with him, changed him, made him a little more untrusting of the world, and of life in general. It was a mistake he wouldn't make twice.

So nothing had changed here—no indulging in Little Miss Sexy Painter. Fantasies were a hell of a lot safer. And having decided that, he let his hand slide beneath the covers and fell back into his heated imagination right where he'd left off.

~

MIA TIED the too-long bottom of the old white T-shirt she wore into a knot above her belly button, reached for the roller, then started painting, using the "W method" she'd seen on HGTV. *Paint a W, then go back over it and fill in the gaps.* She repeated the instructions to herself until she found the rhythm, and then the work became exactly what she'd feared —utterly boring.

But this wasn't about fun and excitement, nor was it about fulfillment—it was about money. And as she smoothed the eggshell-colored paint over walls that had yellowed with time, she at least felt she was doing something that obviously needed to be done.

The good news was that the work would be fairly easy. The tops of the walls curved right into the dramatically high ceiling, which would also get painted, so the only edgework would be around the bar, a couple of doorways, and the dark wainscoting that circled the large room. She stopped for a moment and took another glance around the big room. The truth was—it was a fabulous space full of potential. The antique cherrywood bar was probably older than Aunt Clara's bathtub, and a few nicks only added to its charm.

Sighing, she refocused on her work. *Paint a W and fill in the gaps.* Unfortunately, though, it just didn't take that much concentration, and studying the bar had reminded her of her only other visit here, three nights ago. She bit her lip at the memory of Rick Rose nearly pressing her to the wall with his hard, muscular body.

"Big macho stud," she muttered, rolling her eyes, but the recollection filled her with an undeniable warmth. She'd been sure he would kiss her. Even with a roomful of loud people a few feet away, for a moment it had felt as if they were completely alone. She still didn't know him, but she wouldn't have stopped him.

No, that would have been one birthday present she'd have accepted wholeheartedly.

She'd gone home elated to think he was attracted to her, too—she hadn't expected that. But then again, he hadn't acted on it, so for all she knew, she was imagining the whole thing. Maybe all that heat had been one-sided and staring into those intimidating eyes had only made her see what she wanted to. Maybe his moves had been about just that—wanting to intimidate her. She'd met men like that—who, for no particular reason other than their egos or insecurities, wanted women to know they were in charge, in power. An age-old behavior.

Hell, for all she knew, the leopard-laden Kelly Ann was his girlfriend. She still didn't know if he had one, or maybe even a wife left sitting at home while he was coming on to women in his bar. She still hadn't asked her aunt any questions about him over the weekend, not wanting to let her attraction leak out, but maybe she should have.

Either way, though, having sex with Rick Rose would be a bad move, much more complicated than her little bathtub daydream. Because even if she could play the sexy nymph for all she was worth, even if she could indulge her fantasies and succumb to her body's hungers, in the end, she'd get emotionally involved. And besides the fact that she'd soon be leaving South Carolina behind, one look into Rick Rose's gaze had told her all she needed to know about him. He was everything hot and sexy a woman could want, but he was also the type to slap you on the ass when it over, and send you on your way with a wink and a grin.

She'd shown up this morning to find a key and a note on the door, instructing her to let herself in and get started, so clearly he hadn't been bursting at the seams to see her again —and it was probably just as well. She'd gotten two guys from the hardware store to bring in a couple of ladders and an electric scaffold.

It had hit her just yesterday that they hadn't even discussed what he would pay her for the job. So she'd done a little research on it, but mostly decided to just take what he gave her in the end, whatever he thought was fair. Since— whether he knew it or not—she wasn't exactly an expert at this, and the whole point was really just earning some income—*any* income—on this particular point she was content to just go with the flow, paint the bar, get the pay, and be grateful for it.

Which reminded her, back to work. *Paint a W and fill in the gaps.* But she let out a sigh at the very concept of having to cover this entire place with plain off-white paint. *It's not even a color.* She should have pushed him for a color. Not that she knew him well enough to push *anything*. And he *had* already bought the paint, making it a little late for that.

But she couldn't help thinking that painting this entire place one bland non-color was a pure waste of architecture. High ceilings, original woodwork; she couldn't help thinking the curve where the ceiling met the wall should somehow be accentuated, not just blended in as if it were nothing. Tipping her head back to look upward, she had the sensation that something should be spilling visually from the ceiling.

"What do you paint?" he'd asked her the other night. She could still hear his deep voice wrapping around the words, still feel his dark eyes penetrating her. Despite the answer she'd clumsily given, she'd been thinking something else. *Angels. I paint angels. Dramatic, passionate angels filled with desire.* She wondered now if she'd blushed, just thinking about her art while looking at a man who was certainly no angel, even if she had already suffered the urge to paint him naked.

In her private world on canvas, angels were perfect

images of man and woman, at once pure but sensuous beings, all aching for a union angels simply couldn't have. They reached for each other without ever quite touching, their eyes replete with desperate yearning. They existed in a world of longing not completely understood and never fulfilled.

Sort of like my *life*. The glum thought weighed on her as she glided the roller over a new section of yellowed plaster.

Maybe that's why she couldn't stop painting them. They yearned for a physical connection they could never achieve, and *she* yearned for a connection with others, through her art, that she was beginning to fear she'd never have, either. And as a result of letting that longing mean so much to her that she'd forsaken everything else, here she was now, painting a wall white, turning it into a blank canvas no one would ever fill.

Mia stopped and glanced toward the ceiling once more.

All that space. All that blank space. White canvas.

A blank, empty canvas just waiting for…what?

The idea blossomed inside her almost instantly, clearly—though maybe exploding described the sensation better. One second—nothing, and the next it was all bursting outward in her mind's eye, Big Bang style. Within a few short seconds she understood what belonged on the walls and ceiling of this room, and a surge of creative energy shot through her.

If she was going to be paid for her painting, shouldn't it be *her* painting, her real work?

And if she didn't stop at normal quitting time and toiled around the clock, she could get it done without running *too* late—she knew it.

So that settled it. Lowering her roller of white paint back into the tray with a smile of anticipation, she grabbed up her purse and headed back to the hardware store. Rick Rose would get much more than he was paying for and she'd go away with a much greater feeling of artistic gratification.

~

RICK PULLED his truck to the curb in front of the Rose Tavern, spotted the doors and windows still open, and checked his watch. Five-thirty. Hmm, maybe Little Miss Sexy Painter was a harder worker than he'd expected; he'd been sure the place would be locked up and empty again by now. Of course, this meant he would see her, which hadn't been part of his plan.

But he could sure as hell face an attractive woman without acting on his impulses, and he would prove that to himself right now.

The pungent scent of fresh paint met him at the door as he walked through. An initial glance around the quiet room revealed the requisite drop cloths and paint cans, as well as a fresh coat of white on some of the walls and, when he looked up, the largest part of the ceiling. But that was when he realized something wasn't right.

A steel scaffold nearly reached the high ceiling, so he couldn't tell exactly what he was seeing, but bits of unexpected color—pale pink, black, a deep ivory—peeked out from above the platform stretched across the sturdy-looking lift. And his blood pressure began to spike.

What the hell did she think she was doing? She was supposed to be painting the place off-white. Simple, solid off-white. Nothing more, nothing less. Instead...dear God, was that actually a person's bare leg on his ceiling?

"What the hell is going on here?" he boomed.

"Um—just a second," she called, her voice emanating from somewhere above—atop the scaffolding, he presumed.

"No, not just a second," he bit off gruffly. "*Now.*"

The platform began to descend, lowering several feet before stopping, and then Mia Drake backed down the built-in ladder at the scaffold's end. The longer it took her, the more he fumed, ready to give her a piece of his mind—and as soon as she reached the floor, he cut loose. "What the hell do you think—"

Shit. The sight of her stole his words. She wore blue jeans and a white T-shirt knotted at the waist, smudged with bits of paint that didn't prevent him from seeing the clear outline of a lacy bra through the cotton. She had a silver belly button ring. And her feet were bare.

"What the hell do I think about what?" she asked, looking surprisingly defiant and not in the least worried.

The anger already tightening his chest now tightened his groin, too—and it wasn't anger anymore. Damn, he couldn't remember a time when he'd had it this bad for a woman this fast. Mere toes, a sexy belly button, and a snug, thin tee had turned him hard. He wanted her out of that shirt, out of everything.

And with that one thought in mind, he took a possessive step toward her.

CHAPTER THREE

*M*ia didn't know if he intended to strangle her or kiss her, but she held her ground. *Please let it be the second one. Please just kiss me.* Like the other night, his intense gaze was laced with sensuality and a definite sense of power, and it was enough to send all her cautious thoughts from earlier flying out the window.

When the trill from his cell phone sliced through the air, they both flinched.

He never took his eyes off her, but the interruption stilled him in place—and he let out a heavy breath as he reached for the phone at his belt.

"I'm at the bar," he said into it a few seconds later. Then, "The paint job?" Leaning his head back, he cast a doubtful look at the ceiling. "Uh, the jury's still out on that one. Listen, I'm in the middle of something here—I'll call you later."

After pushing the button to disconnect, he spoke pointedly. "That was my brother, Jace. He wanted to know how the paint job was coming along."

"So I gathered."

After another skeptical glance upward, he turned a steely

gaze back on her. "I had no idea how to explain to him that there's a leg painted on my ceiling. So would you like to tell me why, exactly, you're painting *people* up there?"

For the first time, Mia got a little worried about her decision.

But it'll be okay. She'd just be completely honest, and she'd make him understand. Not that understanding seemed like Rick Rose's forte, but she had faith this would work out.

"I'm not painting people," she explained. "I'm painting angels."

He just blinked. Stared at her blankly. "Angels?" He said it in the same tone someone might say, *Martians?*

"Yes, angels." Then she took a deep breath, along with a step forward. *Here goes nothing.* "You see, that's what I do—I paint angels. This will be a mural that stretches across the ceiling. It'll give the place a lot of character and use the space much more effectively, making use of the great architecture. And I'm not even charging you anything extra."

He spoke dryly. "Well, that's a relief."

She attempted to sell it with a smile. "Your ceiling will be the talk of the town."

Unfortunately, though, he wasn't buying. "What if I don't *want* my ceiling to be the talk of the town? This is a bar, sweetheart. People come here to drink and listen to music and bullshit with one another. Not look at angels of all things."

"Well, that's the beauty of it. Since they're on the ceiling, they won't get in the way. No one *has* to look at them. In fact, you'll have to work pretty hard from down here—lean back awfully far—to see them." She demonstrated, exaggerating the motion. "They'll just be there, hovering up above, if anyone's interested. But they won't interrupt anyone's beer-swilling or chit-chatting. You're getting much more than you planned on when you hired me."

"You can say that again."

His derisive tone made her sigh, but she gathered enough courage to look him squarely in the face. And oh, what a handsome, virile face it was—very easy to look at. Even though she barely knew him, she really wanted to make him believe. In her. In her vision. In her angels. She spoke slowly, solemnly. "You'll like it. I promise."

And she almost could have sworn a hint of regret shone in his eyes when he plainly said, "No."

She took another deep breath, a little caught off guard. She'd anticipated that he probably wouldn't be *wild* about the idea, that it might require a little convincing—but his bluntness left her incredulous. "No?" she repeated. "Just no?"

"Just no. It's a rotten idea."

She took the time for another calming, cleansing breath. "I think you're being narrow-minded."

"It doesn't matter what you think, sweetheart. This is *my* bar. I hired you to do a simple job—now do it. "

So much for calming and cleansing—this time she heard herself let out an irate huff. He was so...curt. Inflexible. Unreasonable. Grumpy.

And *hot*. She couldn't forget that one. In fact, as long as he remained in her line of sight, it would be impossible. No matter how mad he made her.

Somehow, her attraction to him bolstered her, helping her to stay just as aggressive as she'd been when they'd met. So she stood up a little straighter, crossing her arms beneath her breasts. "What if I won't take no for an answer?"

In response, however, his eyes simply widened with a smug annoyance that pissed her off. "Then you'll be out of the job you claimed to need so damn bad."

"Why not give this a chance?" she asked. *Reason with him. Make him get it.* "Why not let me paint the ceiling and *then* decide? If you don't like it, I'll paint over it, no charge." The very thought of doing that ripped a huge gash in her soul, but she felt she had to make the offer to make him take the risk.

"Because no one I know goes to a bar to be reminded of church."

"This isn't like that," she explained. "My angels don't make anyone think of church."

That concept clearly caught him off guard, keeping him quiet for a moment. "That doesn't make any sense."

"Only because you haven't seen my angels," she informed him quietly.

After casting another glance to the leg visible above, his voice went lower, more inquisitive. "Then tell me about these angels of yours. What are they like? Not the kinds you see on Christmas cards or —"

"Oh, no," she interrupted, giving her head a quick shake. "Think...Michelangelo, Botticelli. It's a bold comparison, I know, but I can be a bold woman."

His nod was short, acceptant, as if that last part went without saying.

"Think...romance among angels," she went on.

As his angry expression faded to something slightly more primal then, his eyes began to simmer with a familiar heat that made her insides flutter.

The sensation drove her explanation haphazardly forward. "My angels...want something they can't have."

His voice came so soft it was barely audible. "What's that?"

"Each other. They want each other." She swallowed, her own words echoing fainter, her gaze connected to his by something invisible and magnetic. "But they can't...because they're angels, not humans...so their desires go unfulfilled."

The man before her didn't reply and the two of them stood staring at each other until the five feet separating them felt non-existent. Mia's thoughts mirrored those of a few minutes ago. *Kiss me. Please. I can't stand it.* Even if that didn't make any sense—as little as the notion of angels not being about church made to him. They'd knocked heads on the two brief occasions they'd met, and they didn't even seem to like each other much. Wanting to be kissed by him right now bordered on insane. But she really, truly wanted it. Burned for it. At the moment, she didn't care if it was meaningless sex, didn't care if he took her right here on the drop cloth, walked out afterward, and never mentioned it again. She simply wanted him so badly that she couldn't push it down. Nothing else mattered but having this man relieve the almost unfathomable ache inside her.

"So," she finally said when the silent tension became unbearable, "do you trust me?" She glanced at the ceiling once more, perhaps to remind them both what they were talking about.

"I'm not sure," he said—and then all tenderness fled his countenance. "But go ahead and paint your damn angels if that's what you want to do. Just remember they might not stay there, so don't get too attached to them."

It was like telling her lungs not to get too attached to air. And when Rick Rose turned and stalked from the bar without even another look in her direction, Mia couldn't breathe at all. Every ounce of blood seemed to drain from her body and she reached for the bar to balance herself.

What the hell had just happened here?

He'd told her she could paint the ceiling as she wished, yet the victory somehow felt hollow since he'd done so in anger, and also turned down what she'd been offering with her eyes, her voice.

She knew he'd felt exactly the same as she did—*knew* this time, beyond doubt, that she wasn't imagining it. He wanted her as much as she wanted him—but he'd walked away. Why?

"Damn," she murmured. In the midst of her pleas and her passion, she hadn't even thought to look for a wedding band. She'd have to ask Aunt Clara about that as soon as she got home, once and for all.

But that would be late tonight. Very late. Because she had a ceiling to paint, tortured souls to create and short time to do it in—all while her body suffered and throbbed for Rick Rose. She was beginning to think she had more in common with her angels than she'd ever realized before.

～

RICK FELT like a blazing idiot for storming out of his bar that way, and for not doing exactly what he'd wanted to do with Mia Drake.

And for the love of God—angels on his ceiling? What the hell was that about and why had he told her it was okay? He banged his hand on the steering wheel as he turned onto the two-lane highway that rimmed Sassafras, heading to his brother's place outside town.

He knew who Michelangelo was, but he didn't know if he'd ever seen any of the guy's paintings. Yet he'd given her permission to turn his bar into some kind of goddamn art gallery. Or church. Angels, for God's sake. On the ceiling of a bar? He rolled his eyes and let out a sigh.

When he'd found out what she was up to, he'd wanted to grab her and shake her. He'd also wanted to kiss her. Push her down on the drop cloth and bury himself inside her. Make her see a whole different kind of heaven than the one she was painting up above. But he'd ignored *all* the urges, at least as much as he could.

He felt absolutely adolescent. He was a big boy and if there was something he wanted, especially something free for the taking, he usually helped himself. Yet with her it was different. And crazy. That initial danger he felt with her still lingered—enough to hold him back.

And as for telling her she could paint what she wanted... just like when he'd given her the job in the first place, the words had simply left him, unplanned. He was a smart, decisive guy, not the kind who let a woman lead him around by the nose—until now, it seemed. He banged the steering wheel once more for good measure.

Rick pulled into the gravel driveway of his brother's house, his 4x4 small in the shadow of Jace's eighteen wheeler and a few old oaks draped with Spanish moss. Two dogs circled the corner of the old farmhouse in full stride, barking a warning. His brother appeared on the railed porch in jeans and a faded T-shirt, yelling at the German shepherd and collie. "Rhett! Scarlett! Settle down."

Jace had allowed their mom to name the dogs, much to all her sons' regret. But Jace's girlfriends always thought it was cute, and being a ladies' man, he'd refused to change them before the names stuck and it was too late.

"Come on in," Jace called as Rick slammed the truck door.

Inside, he found his youngest brother, Tanner, more fair-haired than the older Roses, sitting at the kitchen table and still looking scruffy from a day at the construction site. For some reason, it irked him. "You couldn't clean up?"

"When did you turn into Mom?" Tanner asked coolly, but Rick just rolled his eyes and didn't reply as he helped himself to a beer from the fridge. He didn't even know what had prompted his remark, but as the oldest brother, he still felt entitled to make it.

When Jace wasn't on the road, the three brothers tried to get together for dinner once a week, and tonight Jace was grilling steaks on the back porch. The tempting aroma wafted through the kitchen window as they all sat down at the table, beer cans in hand, but it didn't make Rick feel any better.

"Well, for a man who's got a week full of nights all to himself," Jace said, "you seem like you're in a shitty mood."

"I've got a woman driving me crazy," he murmured, shaking his head, and the comment made both Jace and Tanner look up. Rick seldom aired his woman problems.

Because life just went a lot smoother when you kept things to yourself. As for why he'd just walked in the door muttering about his current woes, he could only attribute it to the flame of arousal that still had him on edge and not thinking clearly.

"Is it the painter chick?" Jace asked.

Rick eyed his brother with curious annoyance. "How'd you know?"

"You sounded weird on the phone."

"Yeah, well, if you could see what's going onto the ceiling of my bar right now, you'd sound weird, too."

Jace cracked an accusing grin. "No. I mean you sounded weird like...tense."

"Well, if you could see what's going onto the —"

"No, dude," Jace said with a laugh. "You sounded weird like *horny.*"

Clearly caught, Rick leaned his head back, letting out a small growl of irritation at being so transparent. "Here's the thing," he said, deciding it was no use to deny it at this point. "She's totally hot and each time I've seen her, I...almost can't control myself."

From there, he actually began to ramble a bit, about her being Clara's niece, about giving her the job without having quite wanted to give her the job, about letting her paint freaking angels on his ceiling without having quite wanted to let her paint them, about everything...until it finally occurred to him to shut the hell up and quit being so damn open. For one thing, his brothers sat staring at him like he'd grown horns. And for another, now they'd start giving him a bunch of unwanted advice.

"Sounds to me like a case of good old-fashioned raging chemistry," Jace began, pausing to tip his can to his mouth. "More than just your common attraction. Sometimes that's hard to come by, so I say why fight it?"

"I didn't ask you."

Tanner rubbed his stubbled chin. "It's not like you to turn down a willing woman."

"*Most* willing women," Rick pointed out. "But her parents died in a car accident and she has nobody in the world but Clara."

Jace leaned forward, eyebrows knit, clearly not getting the picture. "So?"

"So I don't want her thinking she has me, too. I don't want her glomming on to me, expecting me to take care of her or something. I'm not into charity cases."

Tanner shrugged. "She doesn't sound like a charity case to me. In fact, she sounds pretty damn feisty."

Rick lowered his voice and shifted uncomfortably, already regretting what he was about to say, since it was something he didn't like talking about and seldom did. "Yeah, well, Tammy didn't seem that way at first either, and look how that turned out."

He caught his brothers exchanging glances before Tanner said, "That was years ago, man." Eight to be exact, now that Rick thought about it.

"Ancient history," Jace added.

And though Rick didn't like admitting this, he replied, "Maybe not so ancient to me."

Jace tilted his head. "Don't tell me you're still hung up on her."

"No," he said, and that was the truth. "But...you know

what happened." He wasn't sure he'd *ever* get over how things had ended. Nope, not so ancient at all.

"So this woman's painting *angels* on the *ceiling*?" Tanner asked, squinting slightly as he changed the subject.

Rick shook his head in disgust. "I don't get it, either. But she'd already started when I got there and she swore up and down that I'd love it, so…"

"So you said okay?" Level-headed Tanner lowered his chin, still sounding disbelieving. "That it was okay to paint angels on the ceiling of your bar?"

Rick let out another sigh. "I know, I know. I have no idea why I told her it was all right."

"Uh, maybe because you wanted to get out of there before you jumped her bones?" Jace suggested.

Rick shrugged. "Hell. Maybe."

"Well, you can't let her do it," Tanner insisted. "You're gonna have to put a stop to that paintjob right now."

"Of course," Jace said in a reasoning tone as he pushed his chair back and headed toward the door to check his steaks, "she sure as hell won't sleep with him after that."

Tanner just shrugged. "Doesn't sound like he's planning on it anyway, so he may as well save the bar from being completely ruined."

MIA'S SHOULDER muscles ached as she eased quietly through the front door a few minutes past ten. The house was silent, but Aunt Clara had kindly left a lamp on. She slipped worn tennis shoes from her feet, thinking that her very bones felt weary. She'd painted for over twelve hours today. Of course, even as she stood there ready to melt into a deep, restful sleep, her veins still hummed with a certain electricity. The passion her angels inspired. Or was it Rick Rose? The line was becoming bizarrely blurred.

She heard the creak of footsteps before Aunt Clara turned the corner, wrapped in a quilted robe and looking relieved to see her.

Guilt set in instantly. "Sorry I'm so late—you didn't have to get up."

Her aunt's usual loving expression stayed in place. "Oh, I don't mind. But I *was* beginning to worry."

Mia sighed. "I should have called, but as usual, I got absorbed in my work and lost track of time. Forgive me?"

The old woman smiled. "Nothing to forgive, dear. Now come in the kitchen and tell me about your day while I make you a nice turkey sandwich."

"Aunt Clara," she said, trailing after her to the kitchen, "you don't need to make—"

"Of course I don't need to. I want to." Her aunt pointed toward the table. "Now sit. Relax. Unwind a few minutes."

Rather than argue, Mia just obeyed. "It turns out," she began, "that the job got a lot bigger than I originally anticipated, and it needs to be completed before the weekend, so I suspect I'll be working these kinds of hours all week."

"My goodness," Aunt Clara said, spreading mayonnaise over a slice of bread. "That's a lot to ask. I'm surprised. Rick has never struck me as that kind of a slave driver."

"Oh, he's not," Mia was quick to assure her. "It's my fault. I just decided to...paint something special, more complicated."

Aunt Clara stopped constructing the sandwich and twisted to face the table, a small smile unfolding across her thin lips. "Your angels?"

Mia nodded, pleased that her aunt was one of the people who truly *got* her work. Though perhaps that wasn't surprising since she had, in fact, inspired it—with a Christmas gift, a coffee table book featuring the works of Botticelli. Sweet Aunt Clara seemed meek and innocent, yet she had no qualms about sending her niece pictures of naked people for Christmas. Mia chuckled inside recalling her initial surprise upon receiving it —but then the book had changed her art, and therefore her life.

"They're very evocative, Mia," her aunt said. "They'll be lovely, I'm sure."

"Thank you, Aunt Clara." As the old woman returned diligently to her task, Mia wondered briefly what Clara saw when she looked at the angels, suspecting there might be more passion to her aunt than met the eye.

"About Rick ..." Mia said then.

"Yes?"

"Is he...married or anything?"

Her aunt's voice echoed from inside the refrigerator, where she now bent loading sandwich supplies back in. "Rick? Heavens no." She rose back up a carton of milk in hand. "Now some years back, he was engaged, and there was a nasty breakup. But I never thought much of that Tammy he was with—no I didn't. Seemed to me she was a rather saucy girl. Other than her, though, Rick's always been a confirmed bachelor."

Part of Mia had almost hoped to hear he was married. A wedding vow would provide an excellent reason to keep her distance, and it would also explain why he continued keeping his despite the clear attraction between them. Now, though, finding out he was available only made her want him all the more. No obstacles stood between them, after all.

Well, none that she could identify anyway. Since she supposed that whatever kept him from making a move on her clearly *was* an obstacle. And despite herself, she found herself feeling stupidly jealous of "that Tammy," and wondering just what had caused their "nasty breakup." What insane responses he brought out in her.

"Why do you ask?"

Mia looked up as Aunt Clara lowered a small plate and a glass of milk in front of her on the table. "No reason. Just curious."

Settling in the next chair, Aunt Clara raised silvery eyebrows. "Have you taken a fancy to him, dear?"

Mia forced out a laugh, nearly choking on the first bite of her sandwich, then took a long swallow of milk to wash it down. "No, Aunt Clara, of course not. I barely know the man." She had no idea why she was lying. And for some reason, a vision of her bathtub fantasy invaded her head just then, along with the imagined sensation of impaling herself on him, being filled by what stood between his legs. As heat filled her cheeks, she lowered her eyes, concentrating on her food.

"He's very attractive," her aunt prodded.

It would be stupid to even deny that. "Yes, he is," Mia agreed around a mouthful of bread and turkey. "But I probably won't be in Sassafras for too much longer, and besides"—she stopped to swallow—"he and I haven't exactly gotten off on the right foot. He's not too crazy about the angels on his ceiling."

Aunt Clara looked thoughtful. "Well…he will be once he sees them in all their glory. You mark my words."

Satisfied that her sexual blush was gone by now, Mia raised her gaze and smiled appreciatively. She appreciated her aunt's support more than she could say. "I hope so."

BY THE TIME he'd left Jace's house late Monday night, Rick had decided Tanner was right—he'd have to tell Mia to nix the angels and get back to the simple off-white color he'd originally planned on. As he drove toward the bar, he couldn't even believe he'd let her cockamamie idea go this far in the first place. His brothers had gotten his head back on straight. Well, at least as far as the paintjob went. As for Jace's suggestion that he quit fighting his desire for Mia, he was dismissing that altogether. In his book, temptation still equaled trouble where she was concerned.

When he arrived, she was gone, her beat-up SUV nowhere in sight, the bar left dark and quiet. Not that he was surprised; it was nearly eleven. Even so, he shoved his key in the lock and went inside. Like earlier, the pungent scent of fresh paint filled his senses and when he glanced to the ceiling...hell, he had to take a step back to get hold of himself.

The scaffold had been lowered and the leg he'd spotted this afternoon was now part of a man...well, a male angel, he guessed. Who was naked. On his ceiling. Jesus H. Christ. He ran a hand back through his hair and let out a heavy sigh.

Of course, he couldn't deny her talent. The guy angel was life-size, as big as him, lounging on a small wisp of a cloud. Wings that looked as if they were constructed of real feathers spread behind him, and he appeared relaxed enough, with one knee casually bent and a smallish penis—on Rick's ceiling, for God's sake—at ease between his legs. Rick's gaze, however, was drawn mainly to the male angel's face, his eyes. Clearly, the guy was longing for what rested across the ceiling from him—only Mia hadn't painted that part yet, and Rick couldn't help being curious to see what the man angel wanted so fiercely.

But shit. There was a naked guy on his ceiling. With wings.

He walked behind the bar and yanked up a tattered phone book from underneath, flipping it open toward the back in search of *Winstead*. He knew it was too late to call, but he was going to do it anyway, going to put a stop to this ridiculousness. Naked angels on his ceiling? He couldn't have it. And he was going to explain that to Little Miss Sexy Painter right now.

Snatching up the receiver on the old rotary style phone behind the bar, which had come with the place, he dialed Clara's number suspecting it would connect to an equally old-fashioned device on the other end.

Then he pushed the button to disconnect before it had a chance to ring.

He wasn't sure why, though.

Curiosity? To see what the angel yearned for?

Or was it a bothersome tinge of compassion for his painter that stopped him?

He lay the receiver gently back in its cradle, then peered at the angel once more—at the desperate passion burning in his eyes. They were blue. Like Mia's.

Tossing the phone book back under the bar, Rick walked out and went home.

CHAPTER FOUR

*T*hree nights had passed. And on each one of them he had returned. Late, after her departure, so he could look at the ceiling.

The first male angel's expression of longing now rested on a woman angel, whose slender hand stretched toward him—but they didn't touch, *couldn't* touch—they lay just beyond one another's reach. A wispy, flowing swath of white fabric draped across her, but it only scarcely concealed her sex, and her pale round breasts were left bare and beautiful. This angel, too, boasted wings of white, feathery enough that Rick swore if he climbed up and touched them, they'd be soft as down beneath his fingers.

Since the creation of those first angels, two more had taken shape. The second girl appeared somehow even more demure than the first, long blond hair falling over her breasts so that only the rosy tips peeked through. She didn't reach for her desired lover, but the look in her eyes said it all. It was a look he recognized, a look he'd seen on Mia. The new guy angel extended one hand in her direction, his eyes fraught with want, but his expression seemed to say he already knew he couldn't have her. His wings were darker than the other angels', the feathers accented with bits of cream and beige. Rick also couldn't help noticing that this angel possessed a considerably larger penis than the other male, which—God help him—actually gave him a laugh.

Jesus, naked angels on his ceiling. And he was laughing about it. How the hell had this happened?

The strange truth was that he'd enjoyed coming in each night, watching the picture, the passion, take shape before his eyes. And seeing the sensual vision of the angels longing for each other had only added to his unwitting desire for the painter.

Now it was Thursday night, and one look told him the bar wouldn't be ready for business tomorrow night. And hell —could he even let people come in here and see the spectacle on his ceiling?

The fact was, he hadn't thought that far ahead. For the last three nights, he'd simply been watching the mystery of her, the beauty of her, the sweet, hot passion of her, unfold. He'd been mesmerized.

He didn't like admitting that to himself—he'd only been this taken by one other woman, ever, and it sure as hell had required more than some paint slapped on a ceiling to make it happen. Yet even now, as he glanced up at the expanding mural, his heartbeat kicked up, the blood raced through his veins faster than normal, and he began to get hard, thinking of her.

Like a few evenings back, he walked behind the bar and looked up Clara's number. It wasn't as late tonight, only a little after nine. As he dialed, he wasn't even sure what he intended to say to Mia. *Get your ass in here and finish this mess so I can open my bar tomorrow night.* Or *I haven't seen you in days and it's killing me.*

One ring. Then two. "Hello?" answered a sweet, older voice he recognized.

"Hi Clara, it's Rick Rose."

"Why, Rick, how are you?" She sounded downright delighted to hear from him. "I hear the painting of the bar is coming right along and I must say, I can't wait to see the finished product."

Did Clara know her niece was painting naked angels on his ceiling? He decided to sidestep that altogether. "Speaking of painting, I need to talk to Mia. Is she there?" And still, even as he said her name, he wasn't sure if he was going to tell her she was fired or that he wanted to fuck her brains out. He was usually a decisive man who followed through on his intentions, but somehow Mia Drake was changing all the rules in his life.

"Oh Rick, I'm afraid she's already asleep. And she's been working such long hours that I'd hate to wake her, poor dear. Can it wait 'til morning?"

He took a deep breath, realizing he felt disappointed. If she'd come to the phone, he wouldn't have fired her. "Sure," he said. "No problem."

Hanging up, he envisioned Mia sleeping and wondered what she wore to bed and hoped it was something thin and skimpy—or maybe, like her angels, nothing at all.

MIA LAY ON HER BACK, brushing thick strokes onto the ceiling, adorning her newest angel with hair the color of midnight. Most of her angels were more fair, but she always followed her creative whims and she'd had the urge to make this male angel darker than most.

Of course, she wasn't an idiot—she knew why she had the urge to paint a dark-haired man. Even without having seen

Rick Rose in four days, he remained prominently on her mind. As absorbed in her work as she'd been, he'd lingered there in the periphery of her thoughts—and sometimes in *more* than the periphery.

At night she fell asleep imagining their bodies coming together, moving against one another, sometimes slow and hot, other times fast and hard. She imagined him kissing and suckling her breasts just before the warm weight of his body pressed into her, just before he filled the empty spot between her aching thighs.

God, she wanted him even now as she lay painting. Her breasts burned for his touch, and so did her sex, held tight and tingly within the confines of old blue jeans.

Rick's ceiling was the best work she'd ever done—she knew it without doubt. And she also thought she knew why.

In her mind, she had somehow *become* the angels.

She'd always connected with them, but never in such a starkly paralleled way as now. She'd known longing before— for success, to have her art loved and appreciated. And she'd certainly known longing for a man. But something about her lust for Rick went beyond past desires—it was new and complicated. Bigger than herself. It defied logic.

She barely knew him, and had yet to exchange a truly civil conversation with him—yet somehow, crazily, this felt like more than mere chemistry to her. And if it *was* only chemistry...well, then she'd never experienced such an all-powerful combination of elements between herself and any other man.

Aunt Clara had mentioned his phone call last night over a quick breakfast this morning, leaving her to wonder what he'd wanted. Her first thought? *I missed it. I missed hearing his voice. And I'm crazy for feeling this way about a man I've barely brushed elbows with, but I can't seem to stop it.* Her second, more rational thought? That he hated her angels and was calling to tell her to paint over them.

Please, God, no.

If that was what he wanted, she didn't think she could do it, despite her promise. She'd rather get in her car and start driving to nowhere and never look back than to make them disappear by her own hand.

~

A THIN RIBBON of irritation had grown in Rick overnight. Thin, but it was getting thicker by the next morning when he climbed in his truck and started the engine.

What had begun as an image of her in his mind, lying in some big, lonely bed, needing a man to wrap around her and keep her warm while she slept, had somehow slowly transformed into…a sense of contempt.

He'd been so absorbed in her painting that somewhere along the way, he'd almost forgotten his fears about her. Yet, suddenly, he was remembering.

It had hit him after his phone call with Clara. *Poor dear,* she'd called her great niece, and it had brought to mind Mia's tragic past, and his original suspicion—that she was one of those needy types, and also a woman who played a part to get what she wanted. Her eyes always dripped with hot willingness, but Rick wondered once again what would have happened if he'd taken her up on the unspoken invitation.

Part of his exasperation—hell, a *big* part of it if he was honest—was with himself. For being so taken in. Even amid his doubts, he'd given her precisely what she'd asked for—he'd been unable to tell her no.

Or, well, he'd given her everything but sex, and the more he thought about it, the more he suspected that wouldn't have led anywhere anyway. She was probably real accustomed to pouring on the sexiness—that kind of charm could get you a lot in this world, and Mia Drake obviously knew it.

Despite the all-too-appealing vision of her in his head last night (he'd decided she wore something filmy to sleep in, sheer and gauzy, to go along with her teasing persona), he felt himself being slowly but surely manipulated. Tammy had possessed the same skill, the ability to make him think exactly what she wanted him to, make him do exactly what she wanted him to, all without his ever realizing it before it was too late. Now, with Mia, he saw himself being drawn in the same way. Drawn in by her art, by lust, and by the intrigue of how the two somehow fit together.

She obviously wasn't the kind of painter she'd pretended to be. In fact, it was all making sense to him now, why she was here living with her aunt—she was some struggling, down-on-her-luck, starving artist. Needy personified.

What really got to him was—he'd only met the woman twice. His obsession with someone who'd barely crossed his path was...disturbing, to say the least. Her and her damn angels had somehow taken over his thought process—but that was about to change.

The weekend was here and he obviously wasn't going to be tending bar, so maybe he'd call up Kelly Ann and take care of the hard-on that had been plaguing him all damn week. But first, he was going to pay a visit to Mia Drake and clear some things up. So instead of heading to the nursery like he did every morning, he drove toward the Rose Tavern.

For one thing, the angels had to go. They'd captured his interest and he couldn't dispute her talent—and there was even a small piece of him that cringed at the idea of painting over them—but it had to be done. They belonged on canvas, not in his bar.

And for another, she had three days to finish the job, three days to paint the place off-white like he'd hired her to. If she couldn't do it, all bets were off, no money would be exchanged, and he'd use the coming evenings to paint the damn place himself.

Despite everything, though, his biggest regret at the moment? That every inch of his body still prickled at knowing he would see her again within a few short minutes.

SHE HUMMED as she painted somewhere above him on the scaffolding. A light, breezy tune he couldn't quite make out, but the airy lilt in her voice crawled under his skin and made his nerve endings tingle. He envisioned her lying on the elevated platform, feathering tiny brushstrokes onto the ceiling. Michelangelo with curves—and the voice of…an angel.

Damn. His intentions were crumbling already.

He looked up, but couldn't see a single sign of her presence—only the humming gave her away. He kept right on staring, though, as if he might see through the wood, as if trying to touch her with his eyes.

Emotion roiled inside him and his groin began to tighten.

Because she was humming? No, it was about a hell of a lot more than humming and he knew it. Instinct told him to leave, now. *Walk right back out that door and she'll never even know you were here.*

Despite his resolve, though, his feet stayed rooted firmly in place.

And even as he approached the lift, then reached smoothly for the lever that would bring her a few feet closer to earth, he knew he wasn't going to yell at her. His chest stretched tight as a rubberband.

Stop, damn it. Stop this now. But arguing with himself did no good. He pulled the lever.

When the plywood began to descend, she gasped. "Hey!"

He didn't respond, but let the scaffold lower a few feet before locking the lift back in place. Then he slowly scaled the built-in ladder on the end. He was working on auto-pilot now, or maybe it was more like surrender. But his *new* intentions had just become shockingly clear to him, filling his every move with purpose.

His first glimpse of her revealed the startled irritation in her pale blue eyes. She still reclined on the wood, a small paintbrush in one hand and an old margarine bowl of beige paint balanced on her stomach with the other—but she'd propped herself on one elbow to see what was happening.

Their eyes met and held, but he never stopped moving toward her, climbing onto the scaffold on hands and knees, suddenly feeling like a cat on the prowl as he came to loom over her. Finally, damn it, finally.

"What are you doing?" Her words came on a breathless sigh as he slowly pinned her to the platform, his nearness forcing her to lay back again.

Reaching for the bowl she held against her paint-smudged t-shirt, he set it an arm's length away—then planted his palms on both sides of her head. "Something I should have done before this whole fiasco started."

Her glare didn't stop him from lowering his mouth possessively onto hers.

The whimper of surprise quickly faded into silence as she went still beneath him, just before he felt the pressure of her warm lips against his. She tasted faintly of chocolate from the candy bar wrapper visible just beyond where she lay. He deepened the kiss, easing his tongue into her mouth, as the scents of paint and chocolate and Mia curled about him, enveloping him.

Her arms closed around his neck, inviting him to slide his body against her lush curves in a way that, up to now, had been nothing but a fantasy. And as her kisses began to consume him, he wondered who was seducing who. He'd fully convinced himself she would push him back or tell him to get the hell off her—despite wanting her more than he wanted to breathe at this point, he'd expected his advances to offend her, make her quit, leave. But instead, her legs parted naturally beneath his, making him groan as he pressed his hungry erection into the thick seam of her blue jeans.

Her quick sigh of pleasure shot through him, turning his kisses harder as he began moving against her to create sweet, hot friction. Damn, he wanted her. Even more than he'd known. All thoughts of driving her out of his bar and his life fled—this was completely about fulfillment now, the stark need to sheathe himself inside her.

He reached for the hem of her loose T-shirt, just above their slow grind, and found soft skin underneath. His hands molded to her and slid slowly upward until they reached lace. Grazing his palms up over her bra, he closed his fingers gently, firmly, over the breasts he'd been dreaming about. The quivery sigh she issued against his lips echoed his own pleasure. Pleasure he wanted more of.

That's when she broke the kiss. "Wait."

It jolted him from the utter abandonment of his senses and he gazed down on her wide eyes and slightly swollen lips.

Okay, now *she's going to do what I expected. She's going to say no, push me away.* And despite the lush perfection in his hands, it was almost a relief—because as he'd lectured himself from the first time they'd met, sex with her would be a mistake. *It's better this way. Frustrating as hell, but better.*

Maybe they'd argue, maybe she'd quit and he could hire a

regular painter. A *man* this time. And his life would get back to normal.

"What?" he said, working to sound gruff. "You want to stop?"

But beneath him, she gently shook her head. "No," she said. "I want to move to the bar."

CHAPTER FIVE

*M*ia relished the shock and heat mingling in Rick's eyes. Oh God, right now she relished *everything*. Despite her request to move, she instinctively arched her back, pushing her breasts tighter into his firm grasp, and squirmed against his hard arousal below, frustrated that he'd gone still.

His voice came like a low-burning flame. "What's wrong with right here?"

"On the night we first met," she whispered, "I imagined us on the bar together. And besides, there are things I want to do to you that will be easier accomplished down there."

His stunned expression remained, even if he was obviously trying to camouflage it. "Okay—that's good enough for me."

His gaze never left hers as he backed slowly off her body, even when he paused to lower a tiny kiss to the denim right between her thighs. She shuddered with all the heat she'd been storing up for him—then after he was gone, moved to the edge of the scaffolding herself. He waited below, his eyes gleaming like two dark embers, heating her up from the inside out.

The second her bare toes touched the drop cloth on the bar's floor, she reached down to pull her T-shirt off over her head, tossing it toward one corner. It seemed insane to wait, to waste time—she'd waited for this long enough. And she didn't know what it meant or why it was happening, but she wasn't going to question it. She wanted it too much. She'd never slept with a guy she barely knew before—but somehow, from the start, she'd known she was powerless to say no to Rick Rose. Nothing in her even wanted to try.

His gaze dropped from her eyes to her breasts, straining against the lace that held them. Then he yanked off his own T-shirt, revealing a broad chest, hard nipples, and a well-muscled stomach, all covered by a thin matting of dark hair.

She was just about to lift her hands to the expanse of his chest, indulge the urge to explore—when he closed the short distance between them in one short stride, using his hips to press her back against the cold steel rungs of the scaffold's ladder. Of course, she felt more than just his hips pinning her there—a column of stone jutted from between his legs. In response, she reached up to grip the rails at both sides of her head, thrusting her breasts forward. Pure instinct. A silent offering.

His hands skimmed quickly up her sides before closing again over the cups of her bra, forcing a small, unplanned cry from her lips at the simple onslaught of pleasure. Then his rough fingers curled around the lacy edges and he gave a brisk tug that spilled her breasts out between them. At the sexy, shocking sensation, impulse took over and she heard herself murmur, "They ache for you."

The words made the erection beneath his jeans throb against her, just once, before he reached around with both hands, grabbed her butt to lift her onto a rung, then lowered his mouth hungrily to one pink peak. As he sucked at her nipple, she let her head drop back and cried out, the sound half pleasure and half pain. Opening her eyes revealed a glimpse of angels—lush and desperate.

Still gripping the side railings tight, she hooked her ankles around them, as well, holding herself onto the steel ladder and freeing Rick's hands. Rubbing his hardness where she wanted it most, up above he caressed and molded her breasts with a skilled touch, even as he continued to kiss them, suck them. She'd never dreamed such pleasure could be found while pinned to a ladder, but the fact that her hands and feet were somewhat constrained to keep her from falling off, only added to the sensation of being fully open to him, and to anything he wanted to do to her. She'd given herself over to the moment, the man, completely.

When one hand dropped lower, stroking her through her jeans, she pushed herself against his fingers as a moan tore from her throat. She'd burned for his touch for so long—or at least it had felt like a long time—and it was more heavenly than she'd dreamed, even through denim.

As if reading her mind, though, he moved his fingers to the top button and flicked it open, then slowly lowered the zipper, a sensation which, in her present position—legs spread and hooked around the scaffold—gave her a thrill of unexpected measure. "Oh God, I want you," she breathed.

"Then let's get you out of these blue jeans." As he moved back, allowing her to step back down onto the drop cloth, his gray eyes shone hot as ever.

She wasted no time in pushing her jeans to her ankles and kicking them off, ready to let him see her, all of her. But then —oh—she glanced down at her faded blue cotton panties with a little hole at the hip.

In her world of scraping to get by, such worn and unexciting things were the norm, and for the first time since this had started, she suddenly wondered what Rick Rose expected from his women. Leopard print with gold sparkles? She went surprisingly sheepish. "If I'd known this was going to happen, I'd have worn better undies."

He gave his head a short shake, his look focused on what she'd just revealed. "I don't give a damn about your undies," he murmured. "I'm just interested in what's underneath."

"Oh," she said, her voice coming husky as her embarrassment disappeared. "Well then …" And she concluded that thought by following the next urge—forgetting about her panties as she pushed them down onto her thighs.

See me. I want you to see me.

Without planning it, Rick dropped to his knees before her, like a worshipper at a shrine. The shrine of Mia. Every fiber of his body hummed with pleasure and anticipation, leaving him almost light-headed.

Cupping the backs of her knees, he slid his palms swiftly up onto her ass, sweet and round in his hands, then sank his tongue into the thin thatch of pale brown curls at the crux of her thighs. Her cry speared him with raw passion as her wet folds parted, allowing him to taste the heat of her desire. Her legs parted, too—she leaned back on the scaffolding once again, her arms extended behind her as she braced herself on a rung.

Repeatedly now they'd ended up back on the ladder when he'd had every intention of seeing exactly what she wanted to do to him on the bar, but that didn't matter—they'd get there eventually. The moment she'd lowered those panties, his mouth had been drawn here, like a fly to honey.

Her underwear was officially a hindrance now, though, so he drew both hands around to the tiny hole at the side seam and yanked firmly, ripping them. She let out a noise of surprise as they fell in a small heap at her opposite ankle, but went quiet again when his palms returned to her ass, squeezing, massaging. He then resumed delivering those long, languid licks up her center, each one ending at the swollen bud near the top.

Above him, she moaned and whimpered and fueled his heat, and he forgot the rest of the world existed. The tips of his fingers played along the center of her ass, soon stroking the tiny fissure there, and what had begun as slow, grinding movements on her part had now become hard, insistent thrusts. His tongue thrust back, and as her breath grew harder, heavier, tangled-sounding, he thought, *Come, baby. Come for me.*

He looked up in time for their gazes to meet just before her eyes fell shut and a low, guttural groan escaped her lips. She jerked against him and he never slowed his rhythm, letting her ride it out against his mouth. He only hoped she couldn't feel him shuddering with the pleasure of her climax, which had somehow seemed to echo from her body into his. Damn, *that* was new.

When she sank to her knees, collapsing against him, he hauled her into his arms. "Are you okay?" he whispered.

"Mmm." Her breath came warm on his neck. "My knees just gave way."

The warmth of satisfaction stole over him as he held her close, her delectable breasts pressing soft and pillow-like against his chest.

He wanted more, though, a lot more, so he didn't wait— he kissed her again, hot and demanding.

Her response was just as enthusiastic, and soon their tongues sparred and he wondered if she tasted herself on his. His hands roamed the smooth arcs and dips of her body until he was raking his thumb across one prominent nipple; his other hand grazed past the curve of her ass and into the moisture below. She was practically purring as he stroked her from behind, and when he slid one finger inside her, she let out a small cry.

Her breath grew heavy again, the way he liked it, and he thought she must be fully revived from her orgasm when her hand snaked down between them to cup the rock-hard bulge still concealed in his jeans. He groaned at the welcome touch.

A moment later, she leaned away from him, wearing nothing but the white bra that now only outlined her full breasts. Damn, they were gorgeous—round, soft, their peaks dark and rosy. He wanted them in his mouth again and followed the urge to reach out—but to his surprise, she grabbed his hands, stopping him.

Biting her lip provocatively, she got to her feet and pulled him up, as well. Then she drew him toward the bar. Ah, ok —finally.

He cast a wicked grin of anticipation—and also of wonder, because he'd pegged her dead wrong every time he'd thought she might be luring him with teasing pretense. He was perfectly willing to let her call the next shots, eager to see what she had in mind.

Still half-dressed, he boosted himself onto the bar. When Mia positioned herself between his legs, he reached to help her up—but she only shook her head and stayed where she was, beginning to slowly caress his thighs through the denim.

He'd been hard since before their first kiss, but this new sensation—her splayed fingers raking their way up his blue jeans, along with the sight of her beautiful breasts hovering just inches above his aching erection—heightened his arousal. When she leaned forward to rain soft kisses over his chest, then his stomach, her breasts pressed into the hard pillar at his crotch. A moan broke free from somewhere deep inside him as he watched her ministrations, drinking in each sensual nuance—the way her hair brushed over his skin, the feel of her fingernails as they dug ever-so-slightly into his flesh, the sight of her body as she bent over him, her pretty ass thrust out behind her.

Just when he was beginning to wonder how much longer he could survive the tender torture, she raised up and lowered his zipper. His cock sprung from its confines, stretching his underwear to the limit, and he waited for her to free him completely, but she didn't. Instead, she ran her palm over his length through the cotton, gently testing the weight and feel of him in her hand—until he thought he'd go mad.

"Please," he rasped.

It was the first time she'd lifted her gaze to his in a long while. "Please what?"

His voice came out shaky. "Please touch me."

He berated himself even as the words left him—he couldn't recall a time when he'd ever begged a woman to do something to him.

But he quit caring when she did it. Seconds after his request, she hooked slender fingers around the elastic band and lowered his underwear.

The way she studied his hard-on was almost enough to make him tremble, even before she ran the tip of one long fingernail from the head to the base. When she took him full in her grasp, he cried out softly, pushed his hands into her hair, and leaned down to draw her into a rough kiss. Afterward, she cast a look of pure wantonness, and without ever taking her eyes from his, let her tongue dart out to lick the wetness from the tip of his erection.

"Jesus," he muttered as another tremor racked his body.

It only got worse when, apparently satisfied with her slow torture, Mia took him into her mouth. Sweet heaven. His breath came slow and heavy as he watched her lips slide up and down his length, each move pushing him further into sensual oblivion. She surpassed any fantasy he could ever invent. He tried not to thrust, but it was difficult and oh-so-tempting. Finally, he whispered, "Stop."

Releasing him, she looked up.

"I don't want to come yet," he explained.

Another wicked expression claimed her as she flicked her tongue across the head one last time—and it almost sent him toppling over the edge, but somehow he held on through sheer will.

When she climbed onto the bar next to him, he was more than ready to regain control of the encounter - yet when he urged her to recline on the polished wood, she resisted. His first impulse was to wrestle with her, to recapture that sense of being in charge. Wen she pushed him to his back, though, he let her have her way—just like he *always* seemed to let her have her way. But dear God, she was straddling him, floating above him, rotating her pelvis in hot, tantalizing little circles—so what difference did it make who was in control?

When she used her gyrations to dab her moisture onto the thick column between his thighs, he was more than ready to feel her lowering herself onto him, wrapping him in wet velvet—only instead she whispered, "Tell me you have something in your wallet."

Jesus, he'd *forgotten*? He *never* forgot. Until now.

"Yeah, I do." Lifting slightly, he wrenched the leather trifold from his back pocket and together they fumbled, suddenly maddened, rushing.

The instant he was sheathed, she sank onto him, taking his whole rigid length smoothly inside her. They both let out a gentle moan at the much-awaited connection, and no woman had ever looked at Rick the way she did just then. Her gaze brimmed with confidence and slow heat and sex, seeming to grab onto the moment and relish it.

She moved on him with a soft, sensuous grind, in the same circles she'd teased him with moments earlier. But she wasn't teasing him now—no, now she was riding him, hot and slow. He reached for her breasts, pushing them upward, squeezing her taut pink nipples between thumb and forefinger, until finally she leaned over and dipped them toward his mouth. He opened for her, took one rose peak between his lips, sliding his tongue around the hard pearl of her nipple even as he sucked, French kissing her breast.

Her breath went ragged and he teetered near explosion. Even as he pumped up into her, he tried his damnedest to hold back. Just a little longer, a little longer. His entire body vibrated like a tightly strung instrument—an instrument she was playing agonizingly well. But soon those strings were going to break; he was going to come.

Her circles got tighter, rougher, as she sought another release. He drew firmly on her nipple and she moved on him with rough urgency—and just when he was thinking, *Please, baby—hurry,* she cried out her pleasure and the force of her thrusts drove him to ecstasy, too.

A rough growl left him as his body was lifted, transported, for a few long, perfect seconds of pure bliss. Then he was back on the bar, his arms closing around her as she settled onto him, kissing his neck, murmuring, "Oh, that was good. So, so good."

"Mmm" was all he could utter as the near-sleep stage struck.

But he was lying on a hard bar and it was the middle of the morning, and realizing that was eventually enough to jolt him awake. "Jesus," he muttered when he glanced over and realized the door was standing wide open and the shade on the big front window hadn't been pulled. Anyone could have seen them—hell, maybe *had* seen them. Shit. Something about this woman totally shredded his common sense.

He leaned his head back in a gesture that felt strangely like concession, a concept he wasn't at all comfortable with, and looking up brought the angels above into focus just when he'd almost forgotten about them. Aw hell. He couldn't deal with the issue of the ceiling right now.

He sat up, forcing Mia to do the same. She was naked and beautiful and sitting on his bar and they'd just had mind-blowing sex and he had no idea what to say.

So he kissed her, softly, just once, and murmured, "Thank you."

After which he thought, *Thank you?*

Damn. *Rose, you're losing your touch, buddy.*

Stepping down from the bar, he disposed of the rubber, then adjusted his underwear and zipped his pants—all the while aware of her climbing down behind him and thinking he should probably be helping her.

But no—he should be doing more than helping her. He should be holding her and whispering things and sharing secret, sexy smiles. *That* was what you were supposed to do after amazing sex. Even if it was only casual. You honored the moment. You acted like a decent human being. Or at least he always had in the past.

Only that wasn't what he did now. Couldn't even make himself. Because suddenly all he wanted to do was get the hell out of here and forget this had happened.

After fetching his T-shirt, he turned to see her pulling on her jeans—without underwear, because he'd torn them. The sight was so arousing he had to look away.

"Well," he said, pulling the shirt on without looking at her, "guess I'd better get to work. People are gonna wonder where I am."

When he pushed himself to glance her way again, the jeans were on and her bra was back in place. She looked as uncomfortable as he felt, combing slender fingers back through her hair. "Um...okay. I, uh, guess I should, too." She was visibly surprised—by his coolness. Understandable. He was acting like they'd just concluded a business meeting or something.

But she was trying to roll with it. And he respected that, appreciated that—even if it made him feel like a piece of shit. Locating her tee in the corner, she bent to pick it up. "By the way, you probably figured out that today's Friday and the paintjob isn't quite done."

He nodded. "Yeah—I, uh, actually came here to yell at you about that." *And to tell you to paint over the angels.*

"You didn't yell," she pointed out quietly.

"No." Say something else. Anything to take the focus off of what he'd done besides yell. "But I really need to get the bar back open."

"I'm really sorry," she told him. "I've been putting in twelve to fifteen hour days, and I'm working as fast as I can, I promise."

Damn it—her tender, earnest expression made him want her again, that fast, despite everything else—and so he knew he had to go, now. And at the same time, he was almost waiting—for the real feelings to spill out, for her to pour on the *when will I see you again?* crap, or to at least ask *what this means?* or *what are we to each other?* He knew all the needy stuff would come before he made it to the sidewalk. It was written all over her face—all that remained were the words.

"I know you're working fast," he said, "but work faster. I'm losing money."

She simply nodded. No excuses, arguments, or needy pleas. Just acceptance. He was an asshole.

"I gotta go," he said, then stalked through the door and to his truck, taking in the light, mid-morning bustle of Sassafras and wondering cynically if anyone had happened past the show taking place in the Rose Tavern over the last half hour or so.

As his truck pulled away from the curb, he thought again

of the damn angels he needed to get rid of—the ones he had just let her resume painting. Even so, there was no way he could tell her right now. He was an asshole, but apparently not *that* big of an asshole. He'd figure out what to do about that later.

For now, he had to go to work, get back to normal. He'd finally given in to his urges, and he'd come away much more satiated than he'd even imagined he could—far better than a quick encounter on the desk would have left him. But this was the end of it—no more.

Even if she hadn't acted all needy, he still knew she hadn't wanted him to go. And that seemed enough of a reason to get as far away as he could.

~

SHE NEEDED TO START PAINTING, but she couldn't make herself get back to work yet. Her mind, her body, wouldn't let her focus on anything except what had just happened. She rested on her knees on the drop cloth just below the scaffold where he'd performed profound personal acts on her. Glancing toward the bar, she quaked anew just remembering his incredible erection. Incredible to look at, feel against her, kiss, taste, have inside her.

They'd done...*everything*. Even more than she'd imagined in her fantasies. It wasn't like her to get so intimate with a man the first time, let alone one she'd just met, nor was it like her to be quite that aggressive...teasing...commanding. But each and every physical connection they'd shared had felt as right and natural as it had shocking and thrilling. Her inner sex goddess had taken over.

Yet just as she'd predicted all along, he'd simply gotten up and walked out.

Which she had decided would be perfectly okay with her,

hadn't she? After all, you do it with a guy you don't know—what do you expect? His class ring?

She still felt sad, though. Because she *wanted* to know him. She'd been so drawn to him from the beginning, and even as physical as the attraction was, it went beyond that. She wanted to know his secrets, his hopes, his desires. She wanted to know if "that Tammy" had broken his heart or if it was the other way around. She just wanted more. And she wanted the sex to matter. It was a curse, damn it—the curse of the soft-hearted female.

He'd seemed almost angry with her when he'd left. Not exactly a ceremonial ending to stupendous sex. But who knew? Maybe it hadn't been as stupendous for him. As usual, the leopard-clad Kelly Ann came to mind.

Still the fact remained—she had to finish painting his ceiling and she had to do it quickly. So, forcing herself up off the floor, she snatched up the old panties he'd torn off her and chucked them in the nearest garbage can in the back room. Then she took a deep breath, raised the scaffolding back to where it had been when he'd arrived, and climbed the ladder to resume her work. As she lay on her back, using her paintbrush to create the mere hint of a few black feathers in the wings of the dark angel, she couldn't stop thinking that even now, having had him, she still felt as desperate as the beings above her.

CHAPTER SIX

*R*ick was leaving the nursery on Monday afternoon when Jace rolled into the gravel lot on his Harley. "What's wrong with *you?*" his brother asked as he removed his helmet. Damn, Rick knew he was easy to read, but this was getting ridiculous.

"Nothing," he groused as he headed toward his truck, realizing even as he spoke how stupid the reply sounded— hell, he'd been biting people's heads off all day.

"You did it, didn't you?" Jace said with his usual, easy grin. "You partied with the painter chick."

Rick rolled his eyes, then looked around to make sure they were the only ones in the conversation. "Keep it down, would ya?"

But Jace just laughed. "Come on, dude. Spill. You got horizontal with your painter."

"And vertical, and perpendicular, and every other angle you can imagine," he admitted, sounding far less happy than such a statement deserved. He got in the truck and slammed the door shut behind him.

"Aw, come on," Jace said, clearly more in response to his

tone than his words as he approached the pickup's open window, "don't you feel better now?"

"My dick feels better. I don't."

"Ah. So that means she was all clingy at the end, wanted you to commit your life to her or something, just like you thought?"

"No," he said shortly, "she wasn't. But I still have angels on my ceiling."

And lust in my heart. He said nothing more, though, before he put the truck in reverse and backed out of the lot.

He'd lied to Jace—his dick didn't really feel all that much better. And he couldn't sleep, hadn't been able to all damn weekend. Visions of their sex had kept playing through his mind like a dirty movie. A really *good* dirty movie. He'd been the star, after all.

On Saturday night, he and Tanner had gone to Mac's Bar on the edge of town. The place was his only other competition in Sassafras, and it was *friendly* competition, but he'd taken some ribbing for not having the tavern open, especially since a lot of his weekend regulars had turned up there. Including Kelly Ann. She'd worn a tight purple micro-mini and rubbed up against him in all the right places. Except they'd suddenly felt like the *wrong* places, because her touches just didn't elicit the same response in him as Mia's had.

"Come home with me tonight, baby," Kelly Ann had purred in his ear. "You know you want to."

Only he *didn't* want to. "Not tonight," he'd said, and she'd moved on to Riley Hawkins and his big cowboy hat, which Rick always thought looked out of place this near to the South Carolina shore.

Now it was Monday afternoon and, God, he wanted Mia again. Wanted her so damn bad he could hardly breathe.

He shouldn't go back to the bar with the intention of having sex with her again.

Hell, he probably shouldn't go there at all, until she was done painting and out of his life.

He should mail her the check and put in some extra dough, enough to get her back on the road and the hell out of Sassafras.

Why? Because you still think she's needy?

Absolutely.

Okay, wait. Change that to maybe. To be completely fair about it.

But if he was being honest with himself here, the problem was bigger than that now. Turned out she had more in common with Tammy than just the tragic past and a potentially needy persona. She made him *feel* things. She turned him weak. He didn't want to be weak for another woman.

Although it was half a mile out of his way, he started making turns toward the tavern. He refused to ask himself why as he drove past. As expected, her beat-up SUV sat parked outside, late day sun glinting off the old windshield. But he kept on driving.

Taking the left turn toward home, he wondered if she was inside his bar humming. Lying on her back. Painting intimate parts of beings too beautiful to be human. He wondered what she was wearing. How late she would work, and if she stopped to eat while she toiled all those long hours.

Any other guy would know at least that much, because any other guy would have had the common decency to make some normal conversation with the woman by now.

But he wasn't any other guy.

MIA PAINTED AND YEARNED, yearned and painted. The two

seemed to go hand in hand these days. And maybe they always had, but the yearning seemed to become more torturous with each passing hour lately. Even now, as she lay on the scaffold, brushing golden yellow swirls onto the ceiling, she ached for Rick between her thighs. He'd filled her so well.

The golden swirls flowed from the head of the female angel desired by the dark angel she'd painted on Friday. Her hair was a riot of messy yellow curls—but much longer than Mia's, and different; she made sure. Because she *wasn't* painting her and Rick. She wasn't.

"Hello," a voice called pleasantly below her. Speak of the devil—or at least it *sounded* like him anyway, albeit in the form of Rick Rose. But she couldn't imagine anything more out of character than him paying a *friendly* visit—well, unless he'd come to fire her or something. The devil was a fallen angel, right? She'd do well to remember who she was talking to here, nice or not.

"Hello," she said back. She couldn't sit up without sticking her head in wet paint, so she reached for the button that controlled the lift, lowering it a few feet, then scooted to the edge of the platform and backed down the ladder upon which Rick had done such delicious things to her.

Peering through the rungs as she descended, she spotted him near the bar, lowering several small white bags there. She was just starting to smell something good when he asked, "Do you like chicken and dumplings?" in his usual detached tone without looking at her.

She smoothed her hands over the bottom of her white tank top, absently wiping off any paint from her fingers. "Uh, yeah."

"Good. It was today's special at Millie's."

She didn't quite know what to think let alone how to

reply—she cautiously approached the bar as he strode behind it.

"Coke?" he asked, grabbing a plastic cup from a stack.

"Sure," she said, remaining on guard.

He lifted his gaze only briefly before returning his attention to squirting soda in the cup. "I know you've been working long hours, and I figured you weren't stopping to eat."

"Not usually. How'd you know?"

He glanced toward the scaffold. "I saw the candy bar wrapper the other day."

"So you brought me dinner?" She tilted her head slightly, still not quite believing.

He gave an unsmiling nod, handed her drink across the bar, and filled another cup—for himself, she guessed.

"Thanks," she said, then started nosing around in the bags.

She'd just started to realize it was dinner for two when he went to the back room and returned with a couple of the bar stools currently stacked there. "Mind if I eat with you?"

Her heartbeat kicked up another notch. "Uh, no."

They didn't talk much for most of the meal, just sat side by side at the bar, and it was somehow both awkward and amiable; his knee pressed against hers as they ate. Every now and then, she glanced into the mirror behind the shelves lined with liquor bottles to catch him watching her—but each time, he looked away. Like they were strangers caught checking each other out. Despite having had mind-numbing sex, maybe they were.

Finally, he peered into the now-nearly-empty Styrofoam container he'd been eating from and said, "Listen—sorry I walked out of here like that on Friday. Didn't mean to be an asshole."

She glanced down, too, the reminder flooding her cheeks

with warmth. She had no idea what to say. "It's okay. I mean…I don't really know you. I…shouldn't have let that happen."

For the first time since his arrival, he turned to look directly at her. Her heart beat faster as she forced herself to return the gaze. His dark eyes were as intense as ever. "Do you regret it?"

She swallowed nervously. "No." It came out too softly. "But I probably should."

"I was out of line even starting it." His eyes dropped again, seeming to focus on something behind the bar. "It's just… ever since we met, I've wanted you."

"In the grocery store," she blurted out, her chest tight with nervous tension and excitement.

"What?" he asked, clearly confused and suddenly forgetting not to look at her.

"You thought we'd met before," she explained. "And we had. We stood beside each other one day in the grocery store, in the produce section."

He tilted his head, then slowly one side of his mouth quirked into a half smile. "Cherry tomatoes?"

She let out a short laugh. "Yes."

"I remember. I remember wondering why you were concentrating so hard on them—they were all alike."

She lowered her chin, feeling oddly demure and embarrassed given the sex they'd had—but still dared peer at him as she bit her lip. "I was concentrating on *you*."

He raised his eyebrows. "Even then?"

"Even then."

The confession caused his smile to fade—to a sultry expression that was all too familiar to her by now. She couldn't begin to pull her gaze away.

Hungry. The word stuck in her mind—it was how he looked and how she felt, and it couldn't be assuaged by chicken and dumplings. Their knees still touched, but suddenly the connection seemed to spark electricity.

"I can't promise you anything," he said, giving his head a quick shake, his voice deeper than before. "I mean, nothing. I mean, I'm not —"

She cut him off, couldn't bear to hear anymore. "I understand that. But the truth is, I'm still dying to…" Oh God, what was she saying?

"What?" he asked. It was the merest of whispers. "Tell me."

She took a deep breath, closed her eyes—then reopened them to meet his once more, the connection hard and unyielding. Why lie? Why not just spit it out? "I'm dying to feel you inside me again."

His look alone turned her weak, ratcheting up the burn of desire spreading low and deep inside her. Lifting one hand to cup her cheek, he leaned in to kiss her, a long, languid meeting of tongues and lips. By the time it was done, her hand kneaded his warm, sturdy thigh. Her whole body tingled with the knowledge that it was happening again—this magic, this mystery of sex with Rick Rose.

Instinctively sliding her hand a little higher up the denim, she leaned in for another kiss, but he pulled back slightly. "Wait."

Recalling her identical protest three days ago, she boldly teased him. "You want to stop?"

The warm grin he gave her was the softest expression she'd ever seen on his face. "Not possible," he told her—but he held up one finger, a silent "be right back," then left his stool to pull down the large window shades, and then turning the lock on the door until Mia heard a pronounced click. "Just don't want to take any chances this time."

She offered a short nod, her voice sounding huskier than usual when she replied. "Yeah, I thought about that afterward."

Gently taking her hands, he then urged her to her feet, after which he drew her into another kiss. Like the first, this one was slower, sweeter, more lingering than those of their previous encounter. His touches this time were less insistent, more gentle, a seductive exploration. His fingertips grazed the sensitive skin of her arms before, leisurely roamed her shoulders, then skimmed down the arch of her back before descending onto her bottom.

Slowly, their bodies came together until his oh-so-powerful erection pressed into the soft core of her desire, escalating her need to something more rough, demanding. Once again, she spared a thought for her angels and all she had in common with them. *But at least I'm getting what I want, what I need. My lover's hands are on me, mine on him.* Not forever —she knew that—and perhaps that provided the reason for her feelings of desperation. Yet she got to have him at least one more time, and she planned to savor every second, every touch, every whisper of his lips across her skin. She didn't think about tomorrow—she could only deal with right now.

As his kisses trailed over her cheek and down onto her neck, she sighed at the sweet, intense pleasure such a simple act could bring and let the heat of it flow through her body like a spill of thick, warm paint.

"I want to lay you down," he whispered just below her ear as he drew her onto the drop cloth spread across the hardwood floor. They sank to their knees amid kisses, and he gently eased her back to the unfurled canvas.

She caught a glimpse of her angels above, but was drawn swiftly back to the joys of earth as he slowly began raising her top, swirling his tongue around her belly button ring, then kissing his way up her stomach. Pushing the white ribbed fabric over her breasts, he sprinkled a thin line of kisses across the ridge of flesh above her bra, turning her breath audible, heavy. His fingers peeled back the top of one lace cup and he had just dragged his tongue slowly across her sensitive nipple, making her moan—when someone banged on the door.

Her stomach jolted. She looked up at him, and he looked toward the noise. "We're closed!"

"Come on, man, I want a beer," a guy's voice called.

"Jesus, Tanner," he muttered quietly, then yelled, "Try Mac's."

"What the hell are you doing in there with the lights on and the place all locked up anyway?"

Looking annoyed as hell, Rick rolled his eyes. "I'm... meeting with my painter!"

The man outside paused, then spoke a bit less loudly. "Oh. Damn. Sorry." Then finally, blessed silence. And she somehow got the idea that the guy outside knew exactly what "meeting with my painter" meant.

"My brother, Tanner," Rick informed her, still balanced on one elbow above her, his face mere inches from hers. His thumb gently stroked her beaded nipple, distracting her from what he'd just said.

But she was interested—given that he'd shared nothing with her about himself until this moment. "H-how many Rose brothers are there?" she asked, her voice coming out breathy.

"Three. Jace lives on a farm outside town connected to the family business and drives a semi truck."

"Family business?" she whispered on a sexy sigh.

"My parents run a nursery," he said, his voice sounding a little raspy, too.

"Oh—um...maybe Aunt Clara mentioned that at some point." She stopped blinked, trying to think amid her pleasure. "I'm...suddenly having trouble remembering."

A low chuckled echoed from his throat. "And Tanner has his own construction company. I'm the oldest," he added.

She let out a breath as he gently squeezed the same nipples he'd been stroking between forefinger and thumb. "Why am I…n-not surprised?" she murmured.

Rick arched one brow, looking half amused and half as if he were daring her to explain herself.

"You have a…very commanding edge about you," she told him, the very words deepening her lust.

A slow, sexy grin stole over his handsome face—just before he dropped a soft kiss on the tip of her breast. A wave of pleasure fluttered downward.

"So do you do this often?" she managed to ask. "Have sex with women in here?" Not in a deriding way—but just an honest question. It was hard not to wonder.

The shake of his head came with a light laugh. "No."

"Then, then…" Oh God, the heat between them. "How did he know? I mean, you, um, could have been doing…anything."

He ran the tip of one finger along the same curve of her breast he'd just kissed. "I…might have mentioned being attracted to my sexy new painter."

She tipped her head back on the drop cloth. "Ah."

"Lift your arms," he instructed, his playful demeanor shifting into his more authoritative tone. Good—she wanted to know him better, but she was also more than ready to get back to business here. She complied with the demand and let him relieve her of the tank top.

When he lowered a kiss to the valley where her breasts met, it was like a star bursting in her chest—then he pulled back for another steamy, I'm-so-ready-for-this look. Or maybe that was simply how *she* felt.

He brushed his thumb over a spot on the cup of her bra that still covered her other breast. "What's this?"

She glanced down to see a smudge of dark turquoise and thought the answer obvious. "Paint."

"You paint in your bra?"

"I used to live in New York City and didn't have air conditioning. If it was over ninety, yeah, I painted in my underwear."

"Now that's something I'd have liked to see." His expression brimmed with sensuality. "Brings erotic visions to mind."

She flashed a curious smile. "Like what?"

He hesitated, then let a slow, teasing expression take over his virile face. "That's for me to know…"

Albeit reluctantly, she let it drop, although she instantly longed to hear his fantasies and would have told him hers—about the bathtub—if he'd asked. She couldn't imagine anything more sensual right now than sharing that with each other. But Rick Rose was obviously not a man to be pushed.

He suddenly seemed insistent on getting their clothes off, working at the zipper of her jeans and pulling them down, along with her white bikini panties when she lifted for him. After he shucked his shirt, he hooked one thumb beneath the strap of her bra and slid it from her shoulder. "Take this off," he said, and she soon tossed it aside. She didn't mind being bossed by him when his demands came with the promise of having him inside her, making her feel as whole and complete as she had the first time.

She lay back and watched, hands behind her head, as he shed his jeans and underwear. Dear God, he was a beautiful man, all hard muscle and sinew. The muscle jutting up from between his legs appeared particularly hardened, the sight of which turned the crux of her thighs warm and weepy.

"Now," he said, kneeling next to her, "close your eyes."

Despite her thoughts of a moment ago, this time she hesitated. She was open-minded and could scarcely think of anything she wouldn't do with him right now—but she liked to see what was coming.

He must have read her uncertainty. "Trust me."

That was a leap, but she let her eyes fall shut anyway, wanting to please him.

She waited for something to happen, but instead merely heard him shifting around her—rustling noises, things being moved. What was he doing? The tension of wondering heightened her awareness, and having her eyes closed made her feel extraordinarily on display. Was he watching her right now? Studying her expression? Her body? Her nerve-endings prickled and her sense of excitement grew; her breasts felt as needy and swollen as she did below.

Then the oddest sensation trailed over one breast, making her gasp. Soft, soft, soft—and very wet. What on earth …? She opened her eyes and the sight before her stole her breath.

Pale pink color arced across the curve of her flesh as Rick used one of her artist's brushes to paint her. The vibrations the simple brushstrokes sent pulsing through her were undeniably exquisite—and then she understood. This was his erotic vision.

Her voice trembled as she tried to identify what he was painting on her. "What…is it?"

"A heart," he said, and she could see it now as he reached the point at the bottom, then came back up to start the other half. He raised his gaze to her with a sexy grin. "What do you think? Do I show any promise?"

A heated smile escaped her, and her words came out in a purr. "Oh yes, Mr. Rose, your work appears *quite* promising indeed. I look forward to seeing what else you can do."

His voice dropped an octave. "Does it feel good?"

Growing quivery inside, this time she could only nod. Then watch. Somehow the completion of the pink heart made her feel as if he'd placed his mark on her, as if she belonged to him now. As if she wanted to.

Next, he reached for a new brush—this one he dipped in the shade of blue she'd been using for her angels' pale, mottled sky, then lifted it to her other breast. When he painted a slow, thin circle around her areola, a thready sigh echoed from deep within her. His brush then looped around the edges of her rounded flesh until she realized he was creating a flower.

"They're beautiful, by the way," he said.

"What?"

"Your breasts."

Immersing the brush back into the can of blue, he painted a wide squiggly line down the center of her belly that sent an incredibly sexy tickle skittering through her. She pulsed between her thighs, aware the wiggling stroke was heading in that direction. Considerately, he skipped the brush over her belly ring, then ended the line just above her pubic hair, finishing by turning it into an arrow that pointed south. She laughed lightly at that—but when he parted her legs and began painting tiny pink hearts on her inner thighs, the sensation nearly undid her.

When she raised on her elbows to watch him work, she found him appearing as deep in concentration as any artist she'd ever known. And—mmm—each little heart he created felt like a fingertip climbing oh-so-slowly toward the center of her need. By the time his brush had worked its way to within an inch of where she throbbed, she'd turned whimpery with lust. "You're driving me crazy," she rasped.

He seemed unsurprised—didn't even look up from his work. "I know."

Somehow the cool, confident nonchalance made her thighs flinch—as if her body were saying, *Pay attention to what I want.* "I don't think I can take much more," she admitted, moaning lightly as a particularly gratifying heart took form. "You've got me so hot."

"I know that, too," he replied in the same unhurried tone, and this time it was worse because his warm breath washed over where she was moist and ready for him. He used one finger to painstakingly trace the outer edge of her arousal, the slow touch making her even wetter. "You're so open, swollen," he murmured. As she shuddered in response, he added, "Don't worry, sweetheart, I'll take care of that for you. Eventually."

She let out a heavy breath, wondering how she could stand to wait even another second—but at the same time loving that he was painting her. She loved the feel of the paint on her skin, she loved the colors, the messiness, the recklessness of it—and mostly she loved that it was coming from him, this man she desired with her entire being.

As he painted another heart a fraction closer to the juncture of her thighs, though, she decided it would be his last.

Sitting up, she snatched the paintbrush from his hand, slapped it down on the drop cloth next to them, and said, "On your back," more forcefully than she knew she could.

He appeared surprised, but not bothered—moreover, he looked positively impassioned. She pushed his shoulders toward the floor, aware that he went easily, and then straddled his hips, ready to have her way with him.

"Careful, you're not dry yet," he said with a teasing grin that nearly shattered her sense of dominance.

She quickly regained it, though, along with the will to torture them both a little longer—but mainly him.

Moving carefully, so as not to scrape her wet thighs against him, she bent down, letting her breasts hover above his face. "Kiss them," she said.

Though when he started to reach for them, as well, she reminded him, "Ah, ah, ah—wet." She used the opportunity to grab his wrists and trap them above his head while leaning even closer. He took the cue then, realizing she meant for him to do it without the aid of his hands—with the tip of his tongue, he took careful turns circling each distended nipple, avoiding the paint that went around them as well. After that, he kissed, then cautiously even managed to suckle her without disturbing the sensual little masterpieces he'd created on her.

The ministrations were almost enough to bury her resolve about making him suffer, but she finally found the strength to pull back, just before instructing him, "Roll onto your stomach."

"Why?"

She smile, since he obviously didn't like relinquishing control quite *that* completely. "Because I said so."

His look challenged her at first, then grew warmer, as if to say, *Okay, I can do this—I can go along with the game.*

Once he lay prone, she reached for one of the brushes, dipped it back in the sky blue paint, and began creating what she hoped would be especially tantalizing little swirls on his firm, round butt. He released a deep groan after the very first.

She started at the roundest part of his ass and worked inward, slowly, slowly, listening as his breath grew pleasingly more labored. After one curling stroke in particular, he moaned, "Jesus." And as her swirls extended toward the center, she swept them downward, as well, until she was painting the little marks nearly behind his balls.

That's when he finally said, "Stop."

Ignoring the command, she painted another, and he responded by rolling roughly over to his back, away from her. When their eyes met, his appeared almost angry. "No more. I'm already too close." Then his voice softened. "Time to get back to *you.*"

Despite her earlier frustration, she didn't argue now. Concentrating on tormenting her lover had somehow soothed her, made her ready to withstand more of his imaginative foreplay. "You're going to paint more on me?"

He gave a solemn shake of his head. "Not exactly."

Her eyebrows shot up. "What does that mean?"

"Lie down and close your eyes."

This time, she didn't balk—she simply bit her lip and did it. This trading back and forth of control had her on a plane of arousal she'd never quite experienced. She wanted to do everything with him, like their last encounter, but she was somehow more patient than before, eager to see what he had in store for her.

A few seconds later, a light, soft, feathery sensation started low on one breast, moving from the outer extremity in slow, teasing circles until finally it swished about her nipple. "Oh," she whispered, "that's like heaven." Easing her eyes open, she found he'd located one of her unused brushes, her largest, softest—the red oxtail with white fluffy bristles. She'd never realized she worked with such erotic tools every single day.

With the paint on her body now dry, Rick performed the same sensual circling motions on the other breast with the oxtail brush. She didn't think she could climax from mere touches on her breasts, but moments came when she wondered if she'd prove herself wrong.

Soon he skimmed the brush down her side, tickly soft, before he spread her legs and, starting at one knee, grazed it up her inner thigh. By the time he reached her center, she was panting uncontrollably—and when he stroked it through her wet, sensitive flesh, she cried out at the sheer assault of pleasure, flowing through her rich and deep.

When she parted her legs for him fully, he took the invitation to rake the soft bristles up, then down, using full, long, languorous strokes that felt like hot velvet against her aching flesh. She moved against it without reservation, ready to take in every sensation he delivered.

"That's right, honey," he murmured above her, still stroking, brushing, bringing that sweet, consuming pleasure, until finally he pushed two warm fingers inside her as well.

She whimpered at the sudden invasion, but it was oh-so-welcome, filling the emptiness as he lifted her higher and higher. His fingers moved as he worked the brush up above and she became lost in the ascent to bliss. "Almost," she murmured. "Almost."

And then she was flying—up, up, up—crying out as her body seemed to shoot through the night sky. And when the sweet, hot pulses finally began to subside, she opened her eyes to see…angels.

Trying to catch her breath, she pulled her gaze down to Rick and pretended she hadn't just had an out-of-body experience that made her want to hold him close and not let go. "I…never suspected you were so good with a paint brush."

He gave her a sexy wink. "Guess I'm just a different kind of artist."

Sitting up, Mia moved to straddle him where he knelt. The time for teasing and hesitation was over and they both seemed to know it. Maybe she *didn't* have to pretend—at least not about the depths of her desire.

They looked into each other's eyes as she lowered herself onto him, taking every glorious inch inside.

There was no more going slow after that—they kissed frantically and moved with urgent need together below; she rubbed her breasts against his chest and he held tight to her ass. Pleasure and emotion swept through her body—and the pleasure she clung to, but the emotion she still tried to push aside.

"I want to make you come again," he rasped in her ear.

She pulled back just enough to look into his eyes. "Close," she whispered. "So close." That quick. The sweet hot friction urged her onward and she rocked harder against him.

"God, I want to make you come so good, want to make you explode, want to make you —"

"Oh—*now*," she breathed as the waves of orgasm struck. "*Now*." And it was exactly as Rick had just hoped aloud—this time it came harder, rough flashes of heat and light racking her body with intense spasms that made her sob.

She was lost in her own private heaven until she heard his deep voice. "Don't stop, sweetheart, don't stop. God, here I come, too." He thrust powerfully up inside her and she kept riding him just as urgently, wanting to give him every ounce of pleasure possible.

Afterward, they rolled off of each other and onto their backs, silent, staring at the ceiling. She noticed both their bodies stained with sweaty paint that had mixed during sex, hers onto him, his onto her. The only sound for a long while was their labored breathing, finally softening.

"So...tell me about you and painting," Rick said without warning, his voice warm in the afterglow of sex.

She kept her eyes on the angels, same as he did. "I've always painted, since I was a child," she began. "I tried to get noticed in New York, but it's a very hard business, and it makes me sad that art becomes *about* business, decisions, money. And still, I yearn for my work to be seen, so it's a vicious circle. When I ran out of money, Aunt Clara was kind enough to invite me here." She turned her head toward him on the dropcloth. "I'm sorry I lied. About being the other kind of painter."

His glance was fleeting before it returned to the mural above, yet he reached out to lock his fingertips around hers. "It's okay."

They stayed silent then for a few minutes, until finally he spoke again. "How do you decide about the penises?"

Letting out a laugh, she turned to him, wide-eyed. "What?"

"The guy angels' penises." He pointed to the first angel she'd painted. "Seems like that guy got short-changed. What did he do to deserve that?"

She giggled again, and found Rick smiling at her. "I just paint them as they come to me," she explained. "I vary the way they look, like real people."

"I thought you told me once that they were supposed to be perfect." He concluded by arching one challenging eyebrow.

She countered with, "Perfection means different things to different individuals. It's in the eye of the beholder."

Then his expression turned playful and sexy. "What if you were painting *me*?"

And for a second, she feared he recognized himself in the dark angel toward the front of the room—but when she realized his gaze rested on her, not the ceiling, she could see that the question was more about sex and ego than anything he'd witnessed on the ceiling.

"Don't worry," she assured him. "If I was painting you, no one would think you have a small penis."

Rolling to face her, he rubbed it against her thigh—he'd already grown hard again and the sensation turned her insides to jelly. "So you like it?"

Their faces were only a few inches apart. She simply cast a smile. "You have to ask?"

"I mean, it's big enough for you?" He seemed too confident for the question to be sincere, but she knew he probably just wanted to hear it.

"Aren't you up on the latest?" she asked, teasing. "Size doesn't matter."

A deep chuckle rumbled from his chest. "That's just a line to appease the guys who are little and the women who are stuck with them."

"You're bad," she said, giggling.

His eyes had turned glittery hot on her again. "But am I big?"

"Yes, you're big. And bad."

"Why don't I show you just how big and bad I can be."

CHAPTER SEVEN

I'm glad you lied about what you paint or I wouldn't be lying here with you right now. Rick kept the thought to himself, though, as he grazed his palm across her smooth stomach. Despite his admonitions and resolve, somewhere deep inside him, he'd *known* he couldn't stay away from her, that he had to have her again. She was so open, so cool and sexy, but it wasn't an act as he'd once thought—it was just Mia.

Every pore flowed with heated pleasure as he gazed on the arcs and curves of her paint-splotched skin, her breasts, her stomach. Parting her legs, he slid his hard length across her moisture until she moaned, then pushed himself deep into the hot, tight glove of her body. Who'd have thought he'd find heaven on a dropcloth spread across the floor of his bar?

Damn, this woman took him places he'd never been before. Even as he attempted to glide slowly in and out, to deliver long thorough strokes that would let each of them savor the slick heat they created together, a sense of total abandon washed over him and made him pump into her harder, faster, with no restraint.

"Oh God—yes," she whispered. "Yes."

It was hardly the first time he'd heard such words from a woman's lips, but when Mia said them, they pushed him to the point of no return. Tremors racked him from head to toe as he came in her, groaning until the last ounce of pleasure melted away inside her.

When he opened his eyes afterward, he felt uncharacteristically sheepish. "That was…faster than I intended."

Her smile held a naughty edge. "Don't worry—I like it hard and fast."

If he could have come again, he would have.

Like before, he fought off the urge to sleep. It would have been painfully easy to give in, to pull her into his arms and drift off with her. But he couldn't. They were on the floor of his damn bar. And she…hell, she made him feel things. Things he simply wasn't going to let himself feel. His suspicions about her had died away, but that didn't mean she was safe. *Kelly Ann* was safe. A woman he could indulge in but then forget about was safe. Mia didn't fall into that category.

Although they lay side by side, facing each other, he let his gaze drift upward. But when it landed on the bared breasts of one of the female angels—hardly a distraction, and more a very sensual reminder of the woman who'd painted it —he forced his eyes back down, even though he didn't really want to look her in the face for what he was about to say. "I should probably tell you…I'm not into relationships."

"I figured."

The quick, short reply caught him off guard. "Why?"

She shrugged, her paint-stained breasts jostling slightly. "I saw the way those women were mooning at you in here that first night. If you wanted a relationship, you'd have one, right?"

He stayed silent, painfully aware that he felt far differently about her than he did those other women.

"By the way," she went on, "are you sleeping with the leopard lady?"

"Huh?"

"The chick in the tight leopard-print dress last Friday night." When he hesitated, she added, "It's no biggie—I'm just curious."

"Sometimes. Occasionally," he replied. His gaze had wandered to her angels again, but he drew it back to her. "Not in a while."

She nodded, appearing content, but to his surprise, he somehow felt he owed her more, wanted to *give* her more.

"I was engaged once."

"Aunt Clara mentioned that. She said it didn't turn out well."

"Tammy came from a rough background, abusive. Both her parents were alcoholics. What it came down to was that she needed...more than I could give her. Emotionally." He swallowed hard on the last word, one that didn't have occasion to leave his mouth often. "She needed somebody to be sensitive and caring, somebody to talk to and listen to her and come running every time she called...and I wasn't that guy."

Again, his paint-splotched lover gave a slight, easy shrug. "I'm sure you were caring. And you seem to talk and listen okay."

But he couldn't help laughing at her simple analysis. "This isn't exactly the norm for me."

"I gathered," she said, offering a grin. "So to what do I suddenly owe the privilege?"

He shook his head, then looked away, uncomfortable. "I'm not sure."

She stayed silent, acceptant. Again, he couldn't help

thinking how incredibly unruffled she was—she took every-thing like it was nothing. Not exactly the hysterical, clingy woman he'd envisioned.

"The thing about Tammy," he said, barreling forward for reasons he couldn't name, "is that when I couldn't give her whatever it was she needed, she started looking for it some-where else. I found her in bed with my best friend."

She flinched, then met his eyes, hers shining with aston-ishment. "God. I'm sorry."

He couldn't say why he'd volunteered the information, but the emotions surrounding those days came flooding back: the sense of betrayal, the utter shock, the anger...and the tears that had shown him something he hadn't liked facing, that he wasn't quite as tough as he liked to think. As tension gathered in his chest, though, he shoved all of it right back into the little box inside him where he'd kept it these last five years. "It was a long time ago," he finished, working to keep his expression masked, his voice even.

She simply nodded, then kissed him, murmuring some-thing to herself. And he couldn't quite make it out, but it sounded like she'd said, "What a stupid girl."

AN HOUR LATER, Rick lay on the drop cloth, looking up. Only now he was dressed, and alone. Mia had departed soon after his confession—damn, what had gotten into him to go spilling that kind of shit to her? Talk of an early day for both of them tomorrow, and her promise that she would have the ceiling finished within two days, had melted away the sexy mood and sent her on her way. He'd claimed he wanted to stay behind and check on a few things, but would be right behind her, turning out the lights and locking up.

He'd wanted her to go, was glad when she had, was glad when the intensity had ended.

Yet now he suffered the faint sensation of being left alone.

He hated dealing with these emotions, feeling as if there was something he wanted but just couldn't have. He hated that he'd told her about Tammy. He hated that he'd even thought about it, that he'd let himself relive that ugly moment of walking into his fiancée's apartment and finding her naked with Rob.

Turned out the guy wasn't such a friend—and when he looked back on it now, it was clear Rob had really been more of a long-time buddy, a guy he'd hung out with since junior high, but not the kind of friend you counted on, the kind who was there for you in bad times, the way his brothers were.

Now Rob and Tammy lived up in Greenville; he'd heard they had a baby. He'd also heard that Rob stayed out late and drank a lot these days. Thinking of them being miserable with each other wasn't the consolation he thought it should be—it only made him all the more sour on the idea of one man, one woman, one life together. Some couples were happy, his parents among them—but it seemed to him that most people got tired of each other, even when it was no one's fault.

As his eyes roamed the heavenly world Mia had created on the ceiling of his bar, he came to a conclusion. He and she were over, *had* to be over, before things went any further, and it was for the best. He wouldn't weaken to her again.

Already his resolve felt stronger this time than before. And it wasn't that he'd had enough of her, not by a long shot. It was that he didn't think he'd *ever* get enough of her, not if he made love to her every day for a year, or ten years, or twenty. Ironically, she left him feeling the exact way he'd feared *her* to be: wanting, and even a little needy. And he wasn't going to live his life that way.

And he was probably wrong about it anyway. It was chemical, not real. If he let this go on, it would run it's course, like all things did—but not before it got painful and messy, before one of them hurt the other. This just cut to the chase and saved the pain.

But as for the angels on his ceiling, there was simply no way he could cover them up. It made no sense to have them there—he was more conscious of that than ever before—yet he couldn't destroy the beauty she'd brought into a place that, quite frankly, didn't see much beauty. The kind that came from within, the kind that filled you up with something bigger than yourself each time you looked at it.

He couldn't give her romance, and he couldn't give her the need that burned inside him—but he could give her the angels on the ceiling.

And, well, maybe *one* thing more.

~

THE NEXT TWO days were pure torture for Mia. To paint was like bleeding. She still didn't know if he'd let her work stay there untouched, and even if he did...God, what had she done? How had she let herself get so wrapped up in this project, this man? The two seemed tied together in her heart now. When she thought of leaving Sassafras, leaving the ceiling of the Rose Tavern behind, a strange, empty sadness overwhelmed her. But it was about more than leaving the ceiling—it was also about leaving Rick. To leave one was to leave the other, knowing she'd never see either again. It already felt like a chunk of her heart was missing.

The *pièce de résistance* on the ceiling were the roses she added. In vibrant fuchsia and bold red, they were the punch of color the space needed. Only a few of them dotted the expanse of the sky, but in each curved corner of the large room, she painted a large brown basket from which a profusion of roses spilled down the wall. The angels were what gave the painting life, but the roses personalized it, connected it to Rick.

On Wednesday afternoon, nine days after starting the job, and twelve days since meeting Rick Rose, she found the number of the nursery taped near the phone behind the bar.

A woman answered on the first ring. "Rose Nursery and Landcaping." Mia wondered if it was Rick's mother.

"Hi. Can I speak to Rick?"

"Hold on," she said, then returned a moment later. "I'm afraid he's unloading a truck right now. Can I take a message?"

Mia caught her breath, somehow both relieved and disappointed that he hadn't come to the phone. "Yes. Tell him the painting is finished at his bar if he'd like to come see it."

As usual, she'd forgotten lunch, so she wandered two doors down to the drug store, where she bought a Payday and a Fresca. Upon returning, she boosted herself up onto the bar to eat the candy, and she'd just swallowed the last bite when Rick walked in. Heat infused her skin at the sight of him.

His eyes fell to the wrapper still between her fingers. "Sweetheart, you've gotta start eating better."

She nodded. "I know. I will. I'll have more money soon." Because the job was over and he would pay her now—this was it. She had a feeling she'd never see Rick Rose again. Lest he witness the pain in her expression, she changed the subject. "Speaking of which, it's done. What do you think?" She held her arms wide and looked up, encouraging him to do the same.

He scanned the ceiling thoroughly, then drew his gaze

back down. One corner of his mouth curved upward, threatening a smile. "You added roses."

She raised her eyebrows. "It only made sense for a place called the Rose Tavern."

As his smile came fully into being, she ached with how beautiful he was. "I like it," he said. "I like...the thought you put into it."

Her heart warmed and she bit her lip hopefully. "So... you're not going to make me paint over it? Or just wait until I'm gone and paint over it yourself?"

He shook his head and relief flooded her.

"Thank you."

At least it would always be here now—at least someone would see her art. And maybe every once in a while Rick would glance up at it and think of her and remember the passion they'd shared underneath

When the moment grew silent and awkward, she took a deep breath and forced out the next words. "Well, guess this is it."

His nod was slow, perfunctory. "Yeah." Then he reached in his pocket and extracted a check, folded in half, slipping it into her hand. As her fingers passed over his to accept it, the payment felt hollow. Money mattered—it mattered a lot, it kept you alive, and she needed to have it—but being paid for what she'd created on this ceiling almost didn't make sense. It had been a labor of love, more than one kind.

"So...what's next for you?" he asked. "Moving on to someplace new?"

It sounded like he wanted her to. And before a couple of days ago, she'd actually been planning to stick around Sassafras for at least a little while longer, to see if she could earn some more cash and hand some of it over to Aunt Clara. But recently, she'd decided she *couldn't* stay. She'd be looking for him everywhere. Keeping an eye out for him every time she left the house. And if she saw him, her heart would break. Hell, it would break even if she *didn't* see him. Either way, existing without him would surely be easier elsewhere.

"Yeah, I'll probably leave. It feels like time."

Liar. She didn't know how she'd fallen for him this fast, but that was exactly what she'd done. Leaving would be difficult, yet it seemed the only way to save herself from a life of hopeless infatuation.

"Listen, I've been thinking," he said, and a bolt of hope stabbed through her—maybe he was going to say he'd changed his mind about relationships, maybe he was going to ask her to stay. "My mother knows a guy who runs an art gallery in Charleston. I thought I'd ask him to come see the ceiling, see what he thinks. If he likes it, maybe he could help you out."

Mia's heart rose to her throat. She was at once devastated by the letdown and thrilled beyond her wildest dreams. Most of all, she was touched by his thoughtfulness. "That would be…wonderful. Truly. Thank you."

More than ever before, she wanted to throw herself into his arms, hold him close. At the very least, she wanted to kiss him goodbye.

But she couldn't. Because if she did, they'd likely end up on the floor or the bar, and despite her plan to take sex with Rick for whatever it was worth, she didn't think she could be that intimate with him again. It would only make parting even more difficult.

"I…should go," she said, pointing vaguely toward the door.

He gave a slight nod. And his eyes said more, but she knew it wasn't enough. She knew she had to get the hell out of the Rose Tavern before she lost what remained of her heart.

So she turned and walked out, and it wasn't until after

she'd gotten in her car and driven away that she permitted a few tears to roll down her cheeks.

~

THE NEXT WEEK was a whirlwind for Mia. On Friday, John Brightman, owner of the Brightman Gallery on State Street in Charleston, had called Aunt Clara's house, asking to see some of Mia's canvases.

The small, tidy man arrived in a late model Mercedes sedan, wore khakis with expensive Italian loafers, and sported a goatee. She felt a bit odd greeting him in jeans and a t-shirt, but he'd seemed genuinely pleased to meet her and truly enthusiastic about her art when she invited him onto Aunt Clara's enclosed sun porch, where she'd been working.

"These are truly inspired, Mia," he'd said after studying the dozen paintings propped about the screened porch. "And your mural at the tavern is breathtaking. If I'd had the time, I could have looked at it for hours."

She'd been absolutely speechless; no one besides Aunt Clara and a few of Mia's friends back in New York had ever seemed so taken by her work or handed out such generous compliments. She couldn't help wondering if it was the emotions that had been coursing through her veins while she'd painted the mural that had given it enough passion to catch John Brightman's attention.

On the spot, he had offered her a showing, after which he'd also invited her to work for him. Clearly, Rick had filled the man in on her financial situation, and it so happened he was in need of an assistant for his growing business.

No matter how she looked at it, it was a dream come true. Not only would she finally get to show her work and maybe even sell some of it, but she also had a brand new job in the field where her heart belonged. She sincerely liked John Brightman and thought she'd enjoy working with him.

After accepting his gracious offer, she'd begun to plan. She'd decided she would go to Charleston right away and use the money she'd made from Rick to get her new life started. She picked up a Charleston newspaper at the grocery store, and a day of phone calls netted her a furnished apartment that was ready to move into and required only a six month lease. If she saved enough to buy some furniture by that time, she could find someplace new. Once she arrived, she planned to spend a few days setting up house, then shopping for some appropriate clothing to wear to work at the gallery. In the blink of an eye, she'd been handed a whole new existence, the sort she'd wished for and envisioned for years. And it was thanks to Rick.

She thought about calling him. But she didn't think she could bear to hear his voice. So instead, she opted to write him a brief note of thanks, *for introducing Mr. Brightman to my work, and for the times we shared while I was here. I won't forget them.* She'd made the world's greatest understatement, but she thought it sounded mature, like a woman who had her act together, the kind of woman she aspired to be. And she'd felt it wise not to say more, lest her heart begin gushing onto the page.

Now, as the sun began to set on her last day in Sassafras, she put the card in Aunt Clara's mailbox and lifted the flag, then turned back to see her aunt wringing her hands on the porch, looking as sad as Mia felt.

How insane for me to have the nerve to feel sad! She wanted to kick herself for it.

But she would miss Aunt Clara, and the quaint southern cottage only a ten-minute walk to the beach, and the little town of Sassafras itself. And she would, of course, lament losing Rick. And those kinds of sadness were normal. What lay ahead would surely take away all her pain if she let it.

"Don't be sad, Aunt Clara," she said as the old woman came to meet her at the car. "Charleston is less than an hour away."

Her aunt nodded complacently. "I know, but I'll miss having you around, and having your angels to look at."

"Well, you can pop into the Rose Tavern any time you want to see them," she said with a wink. Aunt Clara hardly struck her as a barhopper, but who knew—maybe she'd be Rick's newest customer.

"I had rather hoped a romance would spark between you and Rick," her aunt admitted without warning.

That makes two of us. But hoping didn't make it so.

Aunt Clara's eyebrows knit as she went on. "I thought perhaps it would keep you here, close to me."

Before that moment, Mia hadn't quite realized just how much Aunt Clara had come to cherish her presence, and only then did she think about how quiet the house would be without her now, how lonely her aunt must have been before she arrived. She'd felt like a freeloader because of the reasons she was there—without ever seeing that perhaps her great aunt's kindness was more than just kindness, that perhaps she was truly happy to share her home and her life with someone.

"I promise to come see you every weekend. Or you can visit Charleston and see the sights. And, of course, you'll have to come to my showing next month." She squeezed her aunt's hands in hers. "I love you. And I won't disappear from your life, ever. I promise."

The two women shared a warm hug, then Aunt Clara shut Mia into the old SUV, packed to the gills with canvases and easels and clothing, most of which bore at least a few dots or smears of paint.

Her heart welled in her chest as she pulled away, catching a last glimpse of her aunt's flowered dress in the rearview mirror, but she determined not to cry. Tears were useless and she'd put them away long ago, having learned that you could cry an ocean and it wouldn't change anything.

As for the few she'd shed after leaving Rick for the last time, they were just as futile. As was pining for a man you couldn't ever really have. Having his body had been spectacular, but as she'd predicted would happen all along, she'd left wanting more. She was just glad she'd never let him know that. This way, she could remain a pleasant memory in his mind.

Why did that sound so empty, though? A pleasant memory—it sounded so vague, unimportant, seldom thought of.

Her parents came to mind as she pulled up the stop sign at the end of Aunt Clara's picturesque lane. People who were no longer in your life couldn't *be* any more than memories. Her parents were the exception to that—she always felt them with her in a way and thought about them every day, even now. But it was only like that when you lost someone very close to you. Anyone else you parted ways with *was* only a memory—and one that would fade over time at that.

A left turn onto the main road led to Sassafras, a right to her new life. For a brief second, she was sorely tempted to go looking for Rick, just to see him one last time. But just like tears, such a move would lead nowhere.

So she turned right and resolved not to look back.

CHAPTER EIGHT

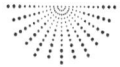

*R*ick dropped the rag he was using to wipe down the bar and went back to the note he'd left lying at one end. His eyes returned to the same handwritten words that kept sticking in his mind. *I won't forget them.* Meaning what he and Mia had shared here beneath the angels. Damn, how he wanted to make himself believe it had been nothing more than sex, nothing more than two people following their physical urges and making each other feel good.

If that were truly the case, though, why was she still on his mind? Why had he picked up this note five times in the last hour since finding it waiting in the mailbox when he'd stopped in to check his liquor inventory? Why did his chest ache when he thought of her? And he'd been thinking of her long before receiving this card.

Setting it back down, he headed toward the storage room to survey the liquor there in addition to what was currently behind the bar. *That's why you're here, remember? For business. Not for pining over a chick you had a little fun with.* And for the first time since unloading the back room of tables, chairs, and bar stools, he thought to empty the wastecan near the door. That was when he noticed the torn blue panties, tossed away like they didn't matter. It wrenched his heart a little harder.

The note said she'd gone to Charleston, was starting a whole new life, and that it was a dream come true. Damn, she sounded happy—and it made him glad. Even if he felt a little lonely somehow at the same time.

Since when do you feel lonely, for God's sake?

It was a totally new emotion for him. Even when all the shit with Tammy and Rob had hit the fan, he'd never felt *lonely*. But the past couple of weeks had held a certain quality of…it was hard to put a word to it, but…maybe it was pointlessness. Life had begun to seem boring. Work had become drudgery. Even running the bar—something he usually enjoyed—had begun to seem a lot more like work than ever before.

It's all in your head.

Or maybe he was wrong and it was all in his *heart* instead.

Stepping back out into the barroom, he leaned back to look at the ceiling. He'd been concerned about how his customers would react, but his worries had been in vain. Some people had the same response as he and John Brightman—they sat and stared at it for a long while. And even those who weren't quite as drawn in seemed to find it sexy as hell. He didn't quite think some of his patrons understood that they were looking at angels—but they read the passion loud and clear. And most guys liked the nudity, which gave him a laugh.

Mia had added so much here in such a short time. Why did it leave him feeling so damn empty?

Moving to the phone, he picked it up to call Jace, who'd just gotten off the road after a week-long run and would likely be in no humor for his request—but that was too bad.

As expected, his brother sounded groggy from sleep when he answered.

"I need a favor. I need you to tend bar for me tonight."

"Can't do it. Gotta get some rest."

Rick took a deep breath. He didn't like to beg, but... "I need this, Jace. It's important."

Need. Lately his life was all about *need*, a concept he'd despised ever since Hurricane Tammy had blown through his life.

Yet, to his surprise, for the first time ever, he suddenly found himself thinking that maybe need wasn't such a horrible thing.

MIA SOAKED in a bubble bath on Friday night, surrounded by the aromatherapy candles Aunt Clara had secretly packed for her. She'd just finished her first week at her new gallery job where the work and atmosphere were exhilarating, but also tiring; she was exhausted and in need of a good long soak. She'd been pleased when she'd discovered her new apartment possessed an old white porcelain clawfoot tub much like Aunt Clara's.

Despite her fatigue, she felt great. Vital. Like someone who mattered, whose life was on the move, and certainly on the right track for a change. A few weeks ago, such feelings were unimaginable. Suddenly, turning thirty wasn't about counting failures and coming to grips with disappointment, but about discovering opportunity, and finding a way to follow her heart, a quest that no longer seemed irresponsible or fruitless. Of course, her thoughts always came back to how she'd gotten here. Without Rick, she wouldn't have any of this.

She gave in to the urge to lean her head back. Her body

felt as weary as her mind, yet she was still keyed up, too, finding it hard to relax despite the "relaxation" labels on the candles. Sliding her palm up her leg beneath the water, she followed the impulse to lift it to her breast. The sensation helped her remember Rick's touch, his mouth, drawing on her nipple. She circled the hard bud with her fingertip, wondering it how it felt on his tongue, and released a sigh as the crux of her thighs turned achy. Letting her eyes fall shut, she began to slip into a fantasy—or in this case, part memory. Rick's mouth gliding over her skin. His rough fingers fondling her where she was hot for him.

Stop it! Don't let yourself think of him like that anymore. It will only hurt worse that way.

Because no matter how wonderfully she was doing, another part of her hurt so badly she couldn't bear it. Upon returning home from the gallery each night this week, she'd quickly thrown herself into painting, having relegated most of the living room to easels and canvases. She'd created new angels who wanted each other but couldn't touch; she'd thrown herself into her work so she wouldn't have time to think about the man beyond *her* grasp.

But wasn't thinking about wanting someone she couldn't have, even if through the eyes of her angels, the same as thinking about *him*?

The loud knock on the door startled her and she flinched, splashing water over the tub's edge. Who the hell could it be? She didn't have friends here yet, and though John had her address, she had no reason to think it was him.

"Who's there?" she yelled. This would have to be good to get her out of the tub.

"Mia, it's Rick."

Hearing his voice was like smashing into a brick wall and crumbling to pieces—nothing could have stunned her more.

Pull yourself together. "Uh, it'll be a minute. I'm...in the bathtub."

She was about to push to her feet and reach for a towel when she heard the old brass knob turn with a click. A second later he came into view through an archway.

"You take a bath without locking your door?" His eyes widened in admonition.

And she shook her head helplessly, still amid the bubbles. "I didn't realize. Totally irresponsible of me. A bad trait of mine."

But by the time she'd finished speaking, he'd come much closer, stopping at the entrance to the bathroom. Some misplaced sense of propriety made her cross her arms, covering her bare, soapy breasts.

"Sweetheart," he said, "I've seen them before."

Already, a familiar heat burned in the dark, beautiful eyes trained on her, and she knew she was looking back exactly the same way. Her voice came out far breathier than intended. "If you want to wait in the living room, I can get out and —"

"No, you don't need to get out. I just need to say some things to you."

"Wh-what?"

She finally let her hands fall from her breasts as he dropped to his knees next to the tub, bringing them eye to eye.

"This isn't easy for me."

"What isn't easy?" She couldn't imagine what he'd come to say. Hadn't they already said everything?

"Mia, I shouldn't have let you leave town."

"Huh?" Her heart beat so hard in her chest that it hurt.

She watched as he lowered his gaze, drew in his breath, then raised his dark eyes back at her. "I thought I didn't want anyone to need me, but I was wrong. I want you to need me. I want you to need me like *I* need *you*."

She lifted one palm back to her chest, soapy fingers splayed in shock. "Rick, I...don't know what to say."

His expression turned from seductive to pained. He took a deep breath, let it back out—but never looked away this time. "That's okay. I...shouldn't have expected you to feel the same." He pushed to his feet. "I felt more than I was willing to admit, and I thought maybe you did, too, but ..."

Mia's hand darted up from the tub to grab his wrist and yank him back to his knees. He looked slightly alarmed at first, but she leaned closer and said, "You're not going *anywhere*."

He looked thoroughly confused. "Why?"

"Because I crave you."

As he let out another breath, this one ragged, the look in his eyes transformed back to the hot, virile one she'd come to know.

"I crave you day and night. I long to have your hands on me. I long to kiss you, touch you. I long to have you inside me. I can't explain what you do to me or what it means, but leaving you was...way too hard." She slowed her pace then, lowered her voice. "I felt myself beginning to care for you, but I didn't let you know because I didn't think you wanted that."

His voice was like warm honey. "Well, I want it now."

Bending over the tub, he took her face in his hands and delivered a sweet, tender kiss. It was far more gentle than any they'd shared before, yet the response it elicited in her body was like wildfire. "Oh," she whispered, stunned, "can we do that again?"

As his mouth moved over hers once more, his tongue eased between her lips, deepening the connection, deepening everything she felt. When the kiss ended, they were both breathless.

"So," he said, "do you think we can make this work, you here, me there?"

She offered a small smile. "It's a short drive."

"You're right. So if you decide to come back and live in Sassafras, you wouldn't have far to go to the gallery." He concluded with a persuasive grin that melted her heart.

Dear God, he wanted her in Sassafras? With him?

Of course she wanted that, too—but she had to be smart, reasonable.

Not that her resolve prevented her voice from trembling when she spoke. "Maybe we should take one step at a time, but…"

"But?" He arched one brow.

"But that sounds like a distinct possibility, sometime in the…future."

His prodding grin returned. "The *near* future."

"You…realize we don't actually know each other very well," she felt the need to point out.

His eyes darkened with heat. "But when I'm inside you, it doesn't feel that way. Does it?"

She bit her lip and shook her head, unable to deny it. Then she couldn't help laughing. Everything in her life was suddenly too perfect to be believed. "Aunt Clara will be thrilled."

"She sounded happy when I called to get your address."

Mia tilted her head. "Sometimes I almost wonder if this wasn't her plan all along. She *knew* I didn't do that kind of painting. She has a secret side, you know."

He looked doubtful. "Clara? Nah."

But Mia nodded emphatically. "I think she has…secret passions."

"Like her niece?" he asked, suggestive expression in place.

Ignoring the warmth that ascended her cheeks, Mia cast a sexy grin of her own. "Did I ever tell you I had a bathtub fantasy about you?"

"Uh, no," he replied, appearing utterly intrigued.

"Well, would you like to hear about it?"

"Actually, I'd rather just make it up as I go along," he said. Then kicked off his shoes behind him and reached for his belt buckle.

She went weak, but found the strength to reach for the top button on his shirt with wet fingers.

Their gazes never left one another as, together, they undressed him, and he soon stepped into the tub, easing into the warm, bubbly water behind her. As she leaned back against his solid warmth, his hands came around to caress her breasts and he rained tiny kisses along her neck.

When his hard, beautiful length pressed into her from behind, she decided that lounging in the bathtub and thinking dirty thoughts about a man she didn't know had been an acceptable way to spend her birthday, but that having the real thing was much, much better.

Thank God Rick was no angel.

ALSO BY TONI BLAKE

≈

The Rose Brothers Trilogy
Brushstrokes
Mistletoe
Heartstrings

≈

The Coral Cove Series
All I Want is You
Love Me If You Dare
Take Me All the Way

≈

The Destiny Series
One Reckless Summer
Sugar Creek
Whisper Falls
Holly Lane
Willow Springs
Half Moon Hill
Christmas in Destiny

≈

~

Other Titles

Wildest Dreams

The Red Diary

Letters to a Secret Lover

Tempt Me Tonight

Swept Away

The Weekend Wife

The Bewitching Hour

The Guy Next Door

The Cinderella Scheme

ABOUT THE AUTHOR

Toni Blake's love of writing began when she won an essay contest in the fifth grade. Soon after, she penned her first novel, nineteen notebook pages long. Since then, Toni has become a RITA™-nominated author of more than twenty contemporary romance novels, her books have received the National Readers Choice Award and Bookseller's Best Award, and her work has been excerpted in *Cosmo*. Toni lives in the Midwest and enjoys traveling, crafts, and spending time outdoors.

Learn more about Toni and her books at:
www.toniblake.com